The Birthday Girls

MIRROR, MIRROR

The Birthday Girls

MIRROR, MIRROR

JEAN THESMAN

AN AVON  CAMELOT BOOK

THE BIRTHDAY GIRLS: MIRROR, MIRROR is an original publication of Avon Books. This work has never before appeared in book form.

AVON BOOKS
A division of
The Hearst Corporation
1350 Avenue of the Americas
New York, New York 10019

First Avon Camelot Printing: July 1992

CAMELOT TRADEMARK REG. U.S. PAT. OFF. AND IN OTHER COUNTRIES, MARCA REGISTRADA, HECHO EN U.S.A.

Printed in the U.S.A.

OPM 10 9 8 7 6 5 4 3 2 1

Chapter One

In some families, a person can ask an ordinary question without launching a string of major disasters. But not in mine. Around this house, a simple, everyday question can lead to absolutely awful messes that can drag on for months, not to mention weird arguments between my parents and ten million birdbrained opinions from my brother, Gary.

For instance, a couple of weeks before my twelfth birthday, I asked my mother if she knew how many babies were born in Seattle on the same day I was, August 25. Simple question, right? She could have said, "Yes, Ceegee, I just happen to know exactly how many babies were born here that day," or she could have said, "No, I don't know." This is what happened instead.

"You want to know how many were born here, in Seattle?" Mom asked. "Wouldn't it be more interesting to find out how many were born in the entire state, or maybe in the whole country?"

"Why do you want to know something like that, Ceegee?" Gary demanded. "Are you hoping August twenty-fifth will be made a national holiday? Like April Fools' Day?" He was nine, and he was having a raisin and mayonnaise sandwich for breakfast, which wasn't half as disgusting as some of the things he ate.

I ignored him. Mom poured more coffee for Dad while he read the classified ads in the Sunday paper. He wasn't looking for anything in particular—he just liked to read classified ads. Sometimes he did it aloud. This could be embarrassing when my friends were there, especially the lucky ones who had normal parents.

"Ceegee, *why* do you want to know about the other babies?" Gary nagged. "Answer me."

"I only want to know about Seattle babies," I said to Mom, while making a big point of ignoring you-know-who by turning my back on him.

"Let me think a minute, Ceegee," Mom said. She filled her own cup. "Somewhere I have the newspaper birth announcement. There were ten babies born in Capitol Hill Hospital that day, I remember that. But I don't know how many there were in the whole city."

"Do you suppose there were as many as fifty babies born on that day?" I asked.

"Yuck," Gary said as he spread another piece of white bread with mayonnaise. "Imagine fifty people with curses on them running around Seattle. Fifty people with big noses and dumb names. Caledonia Giorsa MacBride, Ignatz Pretoria Flugerhorn, Zantor Chickering Mudhut . . ."

2

"Mom, make him stop!" I yelled.

"Dorrie, please put a stop to their argument. I'm reading," Dad said from behind the paper.

"Put a stop to it yourself, oh Exalted Lord Lieutenant of the Emperor's Court," Mom said calmly as she sat down to her breakfast. She, Dad, and I were eating hard-boiled eggs and bacon. Gary was dumping piles of raisins on his sandwich. (Frankly, I think they traded my *real* brother to the trolls for Gary. Nobody human could eat what he does.)

"What exactly do you have on your mind, Ceegee?" Mom said to me.

I sighed. Why do people ask other people to explain their casual remarks and questions?

"I was only wondering how many kids will have birthday parties on the same day as mine," I said as I peeled the shell off my egg.

"Who said *you'd* have a party?" Gary asked. "You told us that you didn't want a party if Molly couldn't be here, and she's going to California."

"We could have a family party, if you're sure that's all you want," Dad said. "Invite your cousins and Grandma . . ."

"How could I *not* invite Grandma?" I asked. "She lives over our garage."

Dad put down the paper. "Believe it or not, Caledonia, I remember that my mother lives here." He picked up the paper again. "Dorrie, somebody's selling a pigmy goat and a llama. Interesting combination."

"We don't want them," Mom responded, sounding a little absentminded. "Ceegee, do you want

3

to have a party after Molly gets back? We could do that."

I shook my head. "No, I want us to go out to dinner and see a movie."

"We can go to Captain Fogarty's Hamburger Grotto!" Gary yelled.

"I'd rather eat dog food," I said. Captain Fogarty's hamburgers were always cold and greasy. Naturally they were Gary's favorite.

Dad sighed and reached around the paper for a piece of bacon. "Speaking of dogs, where's Snickers?"

"You know he won't stay in the kitchen when Gary Gross-out is eating," I said. "He's probably outside throwing up on the deck again."

"Stop arguing," Mom said automatically. She was reading the car ads on the back of Dad's paper.

Grandma, dressed in jeans and an old sweatshirt that said I'm OK, You're A Dink, came in the kitchen door then, and Snickers followed her. "I had waffles," she said to no one in particular. "Snickers ate two of them."

Dad stared down at the dog, who is part beagle and part Lab. Snickers stared back and bared his teeth silently. He never did like Dad much, and everybody knew why but Dad.

"You're too fat," Dad said to Snickers. "You shouldn't eat waffles." He scowled.

Snickers showed more of his teeth and crawled under the table.

"What's new, Anne?" Mom asked Grandma.

"I'm still alive," Grandma said as she helped

4

herself to coffee. "At my age, that always comes as a surprise in the morning."

I get my dark hair from Grandma, and my green eyes, too. She calls them "swamp-green." But I get my big nose from my father. All the MacBrides except Gary have big noses. We have pictures in our photo albums of generations of MacBrides, all with noses so enormous that they cast shadows. You can understand why I don't look in mirrors very much.

Mom told Grandma that we were talking about my birthday. Grandma suggested we wait until Molly came home to celebrate. Gary suggested we forget the whole thing. Dad suggested we go out to dinner at my favorite waterfront restaurant.

Mom said, "I have a brilliant idea."

Dad groaned. "Not again. It's Sunday. Can't I have a little peace and quiet on Sunday? Your brilliant ideas always involve going somewhere and spending a lot of money."

"What's your idea, Mom?" I asked.

"I'm going to find that newspaper clipping that gives the names of everybody who had a baby in the same hospital the day you were born and see if I can't get them all together for a big joint birthday party at one of the parks."

"Oh, great!" Gary cried. "Now I'll get to meet Ignatz and Zantor and Calpurnia and . . ."

"Gary, do you still want to spend the afternoon at the beach?" Dad interrupted. "If that's your fondest hope, stop reciting those stupid names."

"Brian," Grandma said to Dad, "anybody who would inflict the name Caledonia Giorsa on his daughter has no reason to criticize anyone else's fascination with the bizarre."

Dad finally put down the classified ads. "In every generation of MacBrides, there's been a daughter named Caledonia, meaning 'Celtic lass,' and Giorsa, meaning 'grace.' 'Graceful Celtic lass.' It's a beautiful tradition. Your daughter, my very own sister, is named Caledonia Giorsa."

Grandma snorted. "Your father did that to her behind my back. No one ever called her that to her face. Or mine."

"Can we please talk about the picnic?" Mom asked.

"Let's not," I said. "I'd rather hear them argue than plan a picnic that nobody will come to."

Mom looked startled. "What do you mean? Of course they'll come. Think what fun it will be to meet the youngsters who were born on the same day you were and in the very same hospital. You'll make friends for life."

"Mortibelle, Xavier, Figerino," Gary intoned.

"Quiet!" Dad shouted.

Snickers snapped and snarled from under the table.

"Now you've upset the dog," Grandma said. She bent down and peered under the table. "Don't be frightened," she said to Snickers. "You just ignore Brian. That's right. You take that old slipper of his and go right ahead and chew off the heel. That's a good boy."

"What? What?" Dad pushed himself away from the table and reached under it. "He's chewed my slipper! You knew he was doing it!"

Grandma scowled. "Oh, for pity's sake, Brian, calm down. Read the classifieds. There's a nice bit in the personal column about a lost heir. You'll like that."

Dad put his slipper back on his bare foot after examining the teeth marks in the heel. "Lost heir, you say?" He opened the paper again.

"Now," Mom said briskly to Grandma, "let's look in the attic for that old scrapbook of mine and start making lists. Ceegee and her friends are going to have a wonderful twelfth birthday party."

"What friends?" I exclaimed. "Those kids aren't my friends. I've never even met them!"

Mom blinked at me. "Of course you did. You were all in the same nursery together. All ten of you."

Gary nudged me under the table with his bare foot. "Don't you wish you'd said you wanted to go to Captain Fogarty's?"

"Barf," I said. "I'd rather die."

I'd have good reason soon enough to wish I'd insisted on Captain Fogarty's damp gray hamburgers.

Chapter Two

I'll say one nice thing about my mother—well, I could actually say lots of nice things—when she makes up her mind about something, she really gets busy. It only took her a few days to round up five of the families that had children on the same day I was born. The others on the newspaper list had either moved away or had plans that they couldn't break. Or at least that's the excuse they made. They may have already figured out that a birthday picnic at Sandy Beach with strangers couldn't help but be a disaster.

And we *were* strangers, in spite of my mother's cozy little idea that we'd all been great pals in the hospital nursery.

The big day came. I got my presents at breakfast, since nobody thought it was a good idea to have everybody opening gifts at the picnic. Mom and Dad gave me an opal ring and a beautiful jacket. Grandma gave me three books and a subscription to *Defenders,* a wildlife magazine. Gary gave me a package of blank cassette tapes and a candy bar.

We left the dishes in the sink, and the whole family except for Snickers crawled into the van. Snickers didn't care that he was being left behind—he can see into the future, and he knew what was coming.

"We're leaving much too early," I complained from the middle seat next to Grandma. "Nobody else will be at Sandy Park for hours."

"Yes they will," Mama said, "and we have to go early because we're the organizers."

"We've got to stake a claim to the tables we'll need," Grandma said. "If I remember correctly, by this time in the morning there are already people saving tables for later in the day."

"Who cares if we have enough tables?" Gary said from the back, where he was prying the lid off one of the coolers. "It's going to rain. It always rains on Ceegee's birthday."

"It does not!" I cried. "And it's not going to rain today either. The sky doesn't have a cloud in it."

"The clouds come later," Gary said as he chewed on a sweet pickle. "Lots of clouds with thunder and lightning. I bet somebody gets killed."

"Oh, thank you, thank you," Dad said bitterly as he turned the car onto Lake Washington Boulevard.

"Did you all remember to bring your swimsuits?" Mom asked.

"I didn't," Grandma said. "I'm going to find a nice tree and sleep under it all day."

"I didn't," Dad said. "I brought a good book to read."

"I didn't," I lied. "I couldn't find my swimsuit."

"She's got it," Gary yelled from the back of the van. "I saw her roll it up in a towel. But she doesn't want to put it on because she looks so horrible in it."

He was right, but I couldn't let him get away with that, so I leaned over the back of my seat and aimed a slap at him, but Grandma caught my hand. "Kill him later, if the lightning doesn't get him," she said. "I'll help."

I loved swimming, but I'd hated wearing swimsuits for the last year, after I realized that I'd probably look like a skinny gargoyle for the rest of my life.

There were several cars in the parking lot at Sandy Beach, and for a moment I felt a little sick. But Grandma poked me with her elbow and said, "Cheer up. Nothing lasts forever except dental appointments and diets. Even the worst birthday party is better than yogurt and soybeans."

Mom had told everybody to sit at the tables on the north side of the picnic grounds, but no one was there yet. Grandma trotted around quickly; she dropped a blanket on one long table and a stack of beach towels on another, and she divided up the food containers we had brought on two others. We were expecting about twenty people, so we needed to save plenty of room.

Dad began stringing loops of paper ribbons around the area, and Mom distributed paper table covers. Gary and Grandma blew up balloons and tied them to the trees. In half an hour, the place actually looked like the scene of a birthday party. The sun grew warmer. More people showed up, but they only stared at us on their way to other tables.

"Nobody's coming to the party," I groaned, partly relieved, partly embarrassed.

"It's not eleven-thirty yet," Mom said. She checked her watch. "They'll be here. You wait and see."

Gary took his swimsuit and towel off to the bathhouse to change. Grandma helped Mom spread the paper table covers. Dad got a paper cut on his thumb and rummaged through Mom's purse, looking for a bandage.

"Do you need to go to the hospital for stitches?" I asked him hopefully.

He scowled at me. "Of course not. Are you trying to get out of this party?"

"As a matter of fact, yes," I said.

"Forget it," he advised me. "Your mother worked too hard on this."

"She's acting like it's her party," I whispered, so that Mom couldn't hear. "I wish it was."

"In a way it really is her party," he said. He smiled as he watched her. "Mothers are sentimental about babies and parties and all that stuff. So are fathers. You'll have to bear with us and try to get through it the best way you can. You might even have a good time."

"I don't think so," I said. "I want to go home. This is going to be a disaster. And I have a hunch that you're going to tell everybody about my name."

Dad sighed. "All right. I promise I won't. Go ahead and let everybody think we named you Ceegee. You sound like a fast-food restaurant."

I leaned against him, suddenly so miserable that I was sure I'd start bawling in one more second. "I really hate this, Daddy."

He slung his arm around my shoulder. "Smile, for your mother's sake. Look on the bright side. I talked her out of hiring a troupe of folk dancers."

"Oh, she wasn't going to do that!" I cried.

"Sure," he said. "But your grandmother wanted to hire some of those male dancers who don't wear anything but bow ties."

"Are you sure she didn't?" I groaned. "You know Grandma's practical jokes."

"I talked her into doing it on your mother's birthday instead," Dad said. "Look, here come some people now, heading our way."

A heavyset man with a small, red-haired woman and a tall blond boy headed toward us. They were loaded down with ice chests and baskets, and the woman laughed when she saw Mom. "Dorrie MacBride, you don't look one day older." She put down the basket she was carrying and turned to me. "You're Ceegee, right? Happy birthday. We're the Corbetts." She tilted her head toward her son. "This is Chris. He's half a day older than you."

Chris Corbett smiled at me, showing braces. He had nice blue eyes and a cleft in his chin. While our parents talked, he lifted the camera he wore on a strap around his neck and pointed it at me.

"Smile," he said.

"No, no," I said, holding my hands in front of my face. "I hate having my picture taken."

"I take good pictures," he said. "Guaranteed." The camera clicked and Chris made faces at me until I laughed. The camera clicked again. "Happy birthday," he said.

"Same to you," I said, and I meant it.

Another family came, the Wardens. They had a daughter, Jill, with wonderful curly brown hair and golden brown eyes. And a short nose. She grinned when she saw me. "Happy birthday."

"You, too," I said.

"I've never been to this park before," she said. "We live in North Valley."

"It's nice here," I said. "The beach has a sandy bottom instead of rocks."

"Good," she said.

"Yes," I said. I couldn't think of anything else to say.

Chris's camera snapped.

Jill laughed and grabbed me, twirling me around. "Come on, smile," she said. "We're twelve today. It's got to be better than eleven. At least we're starting middle school next month."

"But are we going to like it?" I asked when she let go of me and I caught my breath.

"Probably not," she said. "It'll be really horrible, won't it?" The question was directed at Chris.

He shrugged. "I'll live with it," he said.

A boy had arrived with Jill—her next-door

13

neighbor, she said—and he'd been hanging around, watching us. Jill introduced him as Luke Doyle. He wasn't much taller than I, and he had very dark hair and eyes. He smiled briefly at me and wished me a happy birthday, but he was more interested in the camera Chris was using. They began talking about film. Jill shrugged and grinned at me.

"Let's head over to the parking lot and see if anybody else comes who looks like she's having a birthday today," Jill said. I walked back under the big old trees with her, admiring her gorgeous curly hair and wishing I'd done something—anything!—with mine. Not that it could have looked as nice as hers.

We saw a girl getting out of a car with a woman who was obviously her mother. Both of them had pale blond hair. And fabulous clothes.

"Does she look twelve?" Jill asked me.

"She looks like she's in high school," I said, and Jill sighed.

Then another car pulled in next to the first one. A nice-looking dark-haired family piled out, and sure enough, they had a girl our age, too.

While we watched, the blond girl walked up and said something to the dark-haired girl. We couldn't hear what it was, but it was obviously upsetting, because the dark girl looked down at her shorts and then over at her mother. The blond girl and her mother smiled and shrugged. The dark girl turned abruptly and stomped off in the other direction.

"Nancy?" I heard her mother call after her.

14

"That must be the other girl from Seattle, Nancy Penn," I told Jill. "But she's going in the wrong direction for the picnic."

I was going to run after her, but Jill grabbed my arm. "Maybe you'd better let her go. I've got a hunch that blond girl said something that hurt her feelings."

I looked at the blond swaggering toward us and believed Jill. "What a great way to start a party," I said crossly.

"I know girls like her," Jill said. "They'd rather spoil something than have a good time."

We turned and left the blond girl and her mother to find their way to the picnic alone. They did, and introduced themselves around as Maggie Tracey and her mother from Seattle. Mr. Tracey, the mother said, was in New York on important business and was sorry to miss his daughter's birthday, but blah, blah, blah. I'm sure Mrs. Tracey wanted us all to think that the world would have ended if her husband hadn't been in New York that weekend.

I had a hunch I wouldn't like Maggie, and nothing ever changed my mind.

She looked around and spotted my brother. Gary was wearing his swimsuit, ragged Batman tee shirt, and goggles—and picking olives out of Mom's potato salad.

Maggie said, "Does that little kid belong to your family? He sure looks like you, except for his nose, of course. I'll bet he's glad about that. Not that you're ugly, though. But your brother's almost cute."

15

I was speechless—which almost never happens to me.

Jill cleared her throat. "How nice you could come today," she said to Maggie, but she didn't sound like she meant it.

Maggie eyed Jill's white shorts and orange tee shirt. "Hmm," she said.

That was all. Just "Hmm."

Jill's face turned red. She looked down at her shorts and brushed invisible dust and cobwebs or something off them.

My temper caught fire. I couldn't see that Maggie's clothes were any better than Jill's, but she seemed determined to make everybody feel awful. I wanted to say, "Too bad your ratty old clothes shrank up so much. They make you look like you weren't wearing any and had some sort of disgusting tropical skin disease." But I didn't say one word about her skintight yellow pants and shirt, because Maggie didn't give me a chance. She turned and walked off as if nothing had happened.

"Happy birthday," Jill muttered after her. "I hope you croak before your next one."

Grandma, who had been sitting under a nearby tree reading Dad's book, said, "She's twelve going on thirty," and laughed. "The Traceys are going to be as much fun as food poisoning."

Mom clicked her tongue. "Don't be such a pessimist."

"I'm not a pessimist, I'm just old enough to have learned a few things," Grandma said, settling back with the book. "There are one or two like that at every party."

Jill's parents had brought the birthday cakes, two of them, enormous sheet cakes decorated with all our names and the date. Nancy's parents, a little shy and standing to one side, were carrying a picnic basket and a cooler. Nancy was still nowhere in sight.

Mom bustled over and introduced herself, then asked about Nancy.

"We'll find her," Jill said, and she grabbed my hand.

In the distance, Maggie and her mother stood near the water, watching the swimmers. "I wish they hadn't come," Jill said suddenly. "I've got this awful feeling."

"Me, too," I said. "It's like waiting for a math test to come back from the teacher."

In the parking lot, we saw a Jeep pull in beside the car Jill had come in. "Oh, good," she exclaimed. "Here's Uncle Duffy and my brother, Nick."

The first one out of the Jeep was her brother, who looked fourteen or fifteen. He had curly hair like Jill's, and dark eyes, which he promptly covered with sunglasses. "Kids' party," he grumbled. He stared at me. "Happy birthday."

But Jill's Uncle Duffy hugged her and lifted her up into the air. "Happy birthday, Pumkin," he said, and he rubbed his face against hers.

He was tall and loose-jointed, with longish dark, curly hair, and a wonderful moustache that curled up at the tips. His jeans were ragged, and his tee shirt said Save the Earth. Grandma was going to be crazy about him. I wished immediately that I had an uncle like him. All my uncles were neat and tidy and boring.

Uncle Duffy shook hands with me and wished me a happy birthday, too. But Nick merely gawked at me and groaned.

"He's starting high school next month," Duffy explained. "You'll have to excuse him. From his exalted position, the rest of us are merely dust."

"Go help Mom and Dad," Jill barked at Nick, and he shuffled off, adjusting his shades and shrugging indifferently.

Another car came then, letting out a boy with straight blond hair hanging in his eyes. His parents looked inquiringly at Duffy.

"Follow this young lady to the birthday party," Duffy said, pointing at me.

"I'll look for the girl who ran off," Jill said.

"Who ran off?" the boy with straight hair asked.

"A girl named Nancy Penn," I said.

The boy's parents introduced themselves as the Standishes. The boy was Rod. So everybody was here, I thought. Except for Nancy. I was beginning to worry a little.

Jill took off in the direction Nancy had gone, and Rod, after a moment's hesitation, went after her. "Two can look better than one," he said.

His parents, each with a watermelon, followed me back to the picnic area. Uncle Duffy carried an ice chest. Jill's parents had already gone ahead.

The Big Experiment was about to begin.

Chapter Three

The men decided that the picnic tables should be moved into two rows so that we'd all be closer together. The women—except for Mrs. Tracey—cleared off the table covers, place settings, and food. The men rearranged the tables. The women—except for Mrs. Tracey—put back the table covers, place settings, and food.

Maggie pointed out that one of the tables wasn't level.

Her mother said, "Why do you care? You and I won't sit at that one."

Uncle Duffy found a stick to put under the too-short table leg. He checked it out by pouring a little pop into a clear plastic glass and then fiddling with the stick and table leg until the pop in the glass was level. Everybody thought he was a genius, except Mrs. Tracey and Maggie. They made a big point of sitting at what they called a "safe" table.

Grandma rolled up her eyes and nudged my ribs.

"Let the good times roll," she said sarcastically. I couldn't help but laugh. Grandma could always be counted on to say what I was thinking at times like that. I guess being sixty-five does that for you.

Jill and Rod came back with Nancy. They introduced her to me, and I gave her my biggest smile to make up for whatever Maggie had said to her.

"I hope you brought a swimsuit," I said to Nancy. "The water's warm at this beach. Lots warmer than other places."

She was twisting the ends of her nice brown hair. "I know," she said bashfully. "I swim here a lot."

"So do I," Rod said. "How come I've never seen you around?"

Nancy only shrugged. She sat down next to me, but her wary brown eyes were turned toward Maggie, who was strutting around examining the food—and sneering.

Her expression angered me. She and her mother hadn't brought anything to the picnic, so she didn't have a right to be critical of anyone else's contribution.

"If you kids want to swim before we eat," Dad said, "you ought to start now. I'm getting hungry, and when I'm ready to eat, the party begins."

The men all laughed. Gary and Nick laughed, too. Mom said, "Brian, for heaven's sake, don't rush everybody. I'll give you a sandwich if you're that hungry."

But Dad was right to get us moving. If it had been left to me, I'd have stayed out of my swimsuit and out of the water until the sun went down.

The girls started off toward the women's bathhouse. The guys, except for my brother, headed down the same path toward the men's bathhouse. Gary was already in his swimsuit and trotting toward the dock.

"I bet a million that you diet all the time," Maggie said to me. "Gee, you're the skinniest girl I ever saw. I'm sure glad I don't have a weight problem, because I don't have a speck of willpower. I'm afraid I'd just get fat and stay that way forever."

"Come on, let's hurry and change into our suits," Jill said in the awful silence.

Suddenly, Maggie laughed and said, "What *am I* thinking of? I've already got my swimsuit on, under my clothes!"

And then, right there in front of everybody, she quickly stripped off her shirt, pulling it over her head so smoothly that I bet she'd practiced a hundred times in front of her mirror.

The boys, including Nick, stopped to gawk. Maggie was wearing a bikini top so tiny that I could hardly see it. And I've got very good eyesight.

What was even worse, she looked gorgeous in it. She actually had a chest.

I hope she dies before the day's over, I thought. I brushed past her and nearly knocked her down because by then she had one leg out of her tight yellow pants.

"Hey!" she cried, wobbling and reaching out to grab Luke, even though Nancy was closer.

I marched on—but I did take a quick look back.

The bikini bottom matched the top. It was tiny. Nick, Jill's brother, had lifted his shades to stare.

But nobody smiled at Maggie. Nobody.

I trotted on, with Nancy and Jill behind me.

"If she sneezes," Jill said, "she'll be arrested."

Nancy giggled a little, but her eyes weren't happy.

"Don't let her get to you, Nancy," Jill said. "You look fine. Stop thinking about whatever she said to you in the parking lot."

I looked inquiringly at Nancy.

"Tracey didn't like my shorts," Nancy said.

"She doesn't like anybody's shorts!" Jill said.

Or my nose, I thought. "Maybe she'll go home early," I said.

"I bet she won't," Jill said. "People like her never do."

We changed into our suits and ran back out. Ahead of us, the boys were already tossing their rolled-up clothes under the tables and sprinting toward the dock. We passed Uncle Duffy heading toward the men's bathhouse.

"Oh, good," Jill said to him. "You can keep Nick and the other guys from drowning."

"You bet, birthday girl," he said. He was swinging a red-and-white-striped swimsuit, one of those with legs that come nearly down to a guy's knees. He was weird and wonderful. I had a hunch he'd make the party fun. If anyone could.

I looked out at the water then, and wasn't a bit surprised to see that Maggie was at the end of the dock, posing as if she was waiting for someone to take her picture. And sure enough, some-one was. Her mother.

"If Chris takes her picture, too, I'll drown my-self," I said bitterly.

"You like him?" Jill asked. "He's awfully nice."

I didn't say anything more. I was too busy loathing and despising Maggie—and keeping far enough under the water so that nobody could see that I looked about as gorgeous in my swimsuit as my brother looked in his.

All of us except Maggie stayed in the water for nearly an hour. Maggie lay on the dock in everybody's way, cooking in the sun. The way the boys stepped over her without saying anything to her made me hope that they didn't think she was even half as terrific as she did herself.

Jill's uncle was great, though. He could swim underwater like an eel, and before the hour was up, he'd taught the rest of us—except for Mag-gie—to slither along like that, too.

Maggie wouldn't have dared get her suit wet.

Finally, when most of us were tired, we went back to the tables and wrapped up in towels. Our mothers, except for Mrs. Tracey, hurried around serving everybody.

At my table, my parents and I sat with the Corbetts. Chris was at the opposite end so I couldn't talk to him easily, but he grinned at me a lot—and took a picture of me biting into a huge sandwich. I could have done without that.

At the table next to us sat the Penns, my grandmother, and Jill's Uncle Duffy. Grandma and Uncle Duffy were discussing mystery novels.

23

Apparently they both read the same ones, and they were arguing in a friendly way about false clues, called "red herrings."

Across the grass from us, Jill and her family sat at one table with Luke. Maggie and her mother sat at the other table, along with Rod Standish and his parents. I was pleased to see that Maggie hadn't succeeded in sitting next to Luke, which I'd suspected had been her plan, since she smiled at him so much. He was Jill's neighbor and she'd thought enough of him to invite him to the party, so it was definitely better that Maggie wasn't sitting next to him.

Actually, it would have been a better party if Maggie had stayed in her mother's car. Or home.

After the last piece of chicken had been devoured and all the salad bowls scraped empty, my father (who can be counted on to embarrass me at least once a day) stood up and insisted that everybody sing "Happy Birthday." Everybody did, even we kids who were twelve that day. At the end, Uncle Duffy added, "Cha cha cha," and everybody laughed.

Then the birthday kids cut the cakes. Each of us held a knife and cut at the same time. Uncle Duffy took half a dozen pictures of us with Chris's camera. For half a second, I was so happy that I almost forgot about how I looked.

We ate our cake, some of the boys had seconds, and then we sat there, stuffed, while the afternoon sun slanted under the trees and warmed us. I felt lazy and happy and glad that my mother had planned the party.

Around the tables, people were murmuring to each other, laughing once in a while, and generally enjoying themselves. Uncle Duffy found two sandwiches in the bottom of a sack, and when he learned that nobody wanted them, he said he'd feed them to the ducks in the lake. My brother went with him. Nick, adjusting his shades, muttered that he thought he'd watch, too.

Across from me, at another table, I saw Mrs. Tracey watching Uncle Duffy striding away. She said something about him that I couldn't hear.

"What?" I heard Jill cry, sounding shocked.

My parents turned to look behind them where the Traceys sat at the table next to Jill's family.

Jill's mother got halfway to her feet and then sat back down. Her husband reached out and touched her arm.

Mrs. Tracey leaned forward and said something else, then laughed. Maggie laughed, too, shrill as a squeaky hinge.

Jill got up abruptly and ran off in the direction Uncle Duffy had gone a few minutes before.

"Hey, wait!" I heard Luke say. He followed Jill, calling out her name.

I looked at Mom. She shrugged helplessly.

"I'm going to start clearing up the mess," Grandma said loudly. She stomped across to the table where Mrs. Tracey and Maggie were whispering together behind their hands. "Give me a little help, you," Grandma said to Mrs. Tracey.

But Mrs. Tracey merely smiled and whispered something else to Maggie.

I hate people who whisper behind their hands!

And I hate lazy people, too. Suddenly I was so mad that I jumped up, nearly tipping over the bench.

"I'll help you, Grandma," I said.

"Certainly not," she said. "You're a birthday girl. You go off and have a good time." She snatched at the paper plate in front of Mrs. Tracey, knocking her arm against the woman's shoulder. "Oh, dear," she said. "Did I hurt you? How awful! And I slopped salad dressing on your shirt, too. Well, it looks old. No big loss."

Mrs. Tracey tried to ignore her, but her face turned red. My grandmother is very hard to ignore when she's annoyed.

"Why don't we go watch Duffy feed the ducks?" Rod asked me. He seemed desperate to get away. His parents looked down at their plates with such expressions of misery that I wondered what Mrs. Tracey could have said that upset everyone so. I supposed that she'd made fun of Duffy.

Jill's parents both stood up and began gathering up plates and glasses. They didn't say a word.

It was the most awkward moment I'd ever lived through. Until the moment that came next.

"You ought to stay out of the sun," Mrs. Tracey said to me. "I'll bet that nose of yours gets sunburned the minute you stick it out the door."

I gawked at her. Once again, I couldn't think of anything to say or do. My feet were stuck to the grass.

Maggie giggled. "Mom, what did you say the nurses in the hospital said about Ceegee after she was born? That she looked like a what?"

"They said she looked like a macaw. You know. Those funny-looking birds with the huge noses."

"But I'm sure you're really nice," Maggie said to me. Her smile looked painted on her face.

"Hey," Rod said, protesting. His voice cracked. "Hey."

My skin felt as if it had caught fire. My ears were ringing.

Chris was saying something to me but I couldn't make it out.

"What?" I asked stupidly. He heard! He must have!

"I said how about coming along with me?" he repeated.

"Where are you going?" I asked.

"I thought I'd take some pictures of Duffy feeding the ducks," he said.

But at that moment, Duffy and the others came into sight. So much for that way out.

"Let's go for a walk along the shore, Ceegee," Nancy said. "We can wade in the shallow water."

How much had she heard? Was she laughing at my nose, too? I couldn't tell anything from her expression. But I went with her, and Chris trailed behind.

"Where are you going?" my brother yelled.

Chris turned back. "Come on, Gary," he called out.

He was waiting for my brother, but I ploughed blindly on, with Nancy close beside me.

"I hate Maggie Tracey. And I hardly even know her." Nancy said bitterly. "I wish she hadn't come."

27

I know that she was thinking the same thing I was—nothing could be worse than what had happened so far.

Boy, were we wrong.

Chapter Four

I really liked Nancy and Jill. The birthday boys, Rod and Chris, were nice, too. But by the middle of that afternoon, I felt a bond with the girls every bit as strong as the one I had with my best old pal, Molly. And I knew that Molly would like these girls, too.

But Maggie was something else. I couldn't understand why she and her mother had bothered coming to the picnic. Usually I got along with nearly everybody, but I couldn't even remember a time when I'd hated anybody as much as I hated Maggie and her mother.

It wasn't just because of what they'd said about my nose, either. There was something else going on at the birthday picnic, something mean. I knew Maggie had made a crack of some sort to Jill about her Uncle Duffy, who was the most popular person there. And she'd insulted Nancy in the parking lot as soon as she got out of her car. In other words, Maggie seemed to be doing her best to ruin her own birthday. It didn't make any sense. It was as if the only way she and her mother could have a good time was to give someone else a bad one.

But I had this feeling that Maggie wasn't done yet. And I was right.

Nancy and I wandered back to the tables and found everybody else there, waiting for Grandma to finish slicing the watermelons. But people were sitting in different places—Maggie and her mother now had a table all to themselves. Mrs. Tracey was talking about the clothes she was planning to buy the next day in such a loud voice that everybody could hear her. I don't imagine there was anybody left who wanted to sit within a mile of them. Most of the others talked and laughed among themselves—but things had changed somehow. It seemed to me that they were only pretending to enjoy themselves.

Jill and her uncle had sprawled on the grass at the edge of the picnic area. I wondered if they had deliberately separated themselves from the others. I could have been imagining things, though. Duffy was reading a book and he didn't look upset exactly. He looked more like somebody who'd decided that he'd rather be somewhere else but was determined to be a good sport and make the best of things. Jill's eyes were closed, but I was sure she wasn't asleep. Her fists were clenched at her sides and her mouth was set in a tight line.

The sun, halfway down the sky, shone directly on the picnic area. It was hot there, really hot.

"What happens if I eat three pieces of watermelon and then go back in the water?" my brother asked Jill's brother, Nick.

Nick raised his shades a little and stared at Gary. "You cramp up and die, kid."

"Have one piece of watermelon and live, sweetie," Grandma said. She passed a slice of melon to my brother.

I don't think anybody except Gary was particularly hungry. I know I wasn't. I ate half my slice, threw the rest in the trash, and asked Nancy and Jill if they wanted to go wading in the lake with me.

I never for a moment considered asking that creep Maggie to join us, and I didn't care what she thought. The other girls and I found a place where the shallows weren't too crowded with little kids and their mamas, and we waded out until the water reached our waists.

Nancy leaned back into the water and floated. "This is great. I could stay here like this until dark."

Jill bobbed up and down, ducking herself neck-deep. "It's warm as bath water."

I splashed water on my shoulders where sunburn was beginning to sting and sighed with pleasure.

"Hey, Ceegee, don't do that," Jill said. "You'll burn even worse. Get down under the water."

I took a couple of steps out into deeper water and ducked down. "Perfect," I said.

"This whole day has been perfect," Nancy said. "Well, almost."

31

I knew what she meant, and I bet Jill did, too.

We puddled around in the lake, talking about movies, music, and our schools. Jill was starting at a middle school in a suburb of Seattle and had mixed feelings about it. It might be fun, she said, but it might be awful, too.

Nancy lived in Seattle and would be starting middle school, too. We all agreed that elementary school hadn't been half bad. Sort of comfortable. Certainly being one of the oldest kids in school had had advantages.

In the distance, I could hear my brother and Nick yelling and laughing. I glanced over toward the dock and caught a quick glimpse of Chris diving off the board at the end. Rod was just climbing the ladder.

Everything was so nice, so peaceful.

And then I looked at the strip of beach closest to us and saw Maggie watching us. She was too far away for me to read her expression, but I had a strong feeling that she was angry because she'd been left out. Too bad, I thought. You had a chance to be our friend and you decided to be an enemy instead.

I didn't say anything to Jill and Nancy. I swung around in the water so that my back was to Maggie. But I wasn't having fun anymore. Suddenly I'd remembered my huge, ugly nose and the Traceys' nasty comments. I ducked down and held my breath as long as I could, trying to distract myself. But even half drowning myself didn't get Maggie off my mind.

We rested in the water until Jill's mother

called her in. Maggie wasn't at the shore then, and I didn't see her until we got out of the water and walked up the grassy slope to our tables.

The mothers—except for Mrs. Tracey, of course—had cut the last of the birthday cakes into small pieces and had served them with lemonade. The boys, towels slung around their necks and water drops glistening on their backs, were waiting for us impatiently. Chris, as usual, had his camera ready.

"What took you so long?" Nick complained to his sister.

"I'm only getting older, not faster," Jill said, laughing.

"Let's toast the birthday kids," Jill's father said. He raised his lemonade, wished us the best year we'd ever had, and when Chris snapped his camera, everybody cheered.

A few minutes later, as I was scraping the last of the frosting off my plate, Mrs. Tracey called out something from the table opposite me.

"What did you say?" Mom called back.

"I asked if you knew whatever happened to the baby whose mother died that day we were all in the hospital," Mrs. Tracey repeated.

Mom looked bewildered. "I don't remember anything about anyone dying."

At the table closest to ours, Mrs. Warden said, "I do, now that she mentions it. Gosh, it's been years since I thought of it."

"What happened?" Jill asked her mother.

Mrs. Warden shrugged. "I don't think I ever knew the details."

My mother shook her head. "I'd have remembered if I'd heard anything like that." She hesitated, then added, "But then, I didn't get to the hospital until ten that night. Ceegee was born at a quarter to twelve and we went home late the next afternoon. I wasn't there very long, and so I suppose . . ." Her voice trailed off and she blinked, as if she was trying to keep away tears.

"Jill's about fourteen hours older than Ceegee," Mrs. Warden said. "I can remember vaguely that something awful happened that day, but . . ." Her voice trailed off. "How sad. I wonder who it was."

"I don't remember anyone dying!" Rod's mother, Mrs. Standish, said angrily. She glared at Mrs. Tracey. I thought that she might say something else, but her husband put his hand on her arm and shook his head a little. Mrs. Standish looked down at her plate, biting her lips. Mr. Standish glared at Mrs. Tracey.

Mrs. Corbett, Chris's mother, said, "I remember. But I don't recall the woman's name, or even if her baby lived. Hey, let's drop the subject. It's too sad for a day like this. We're supposed to be celebrating."

But Mrs. Tracey said, "I saved the newspaper birth announcement. In fact, I brought it with me. I'm sure the parents will be listed on it, no matter what happened to the mother." She rummaged around in her purse, and finally pulled out an envelope. "I'll read off the names and we'll see if anybody remembers anything." She took a piece of folded newspaper out of the envelope.

34

"Put that back in your purse," Mr. Penn said abruptly. "You're spoiling the party for the kids."

"Yes, let's play a little softball and work off that cake," my dad said. He got up and handed Gary the car keys. "Do your dad a favor and get the ball and bat out of the trunk while the other kids change into their clothes."

But Mrs. Tracey, on her feet now, persisted. "It'll only take a second to go over this," she said. She started reading off names in alphabetical order. "Mary Elizabeth and James Anderson, girl . . ."

"Stop," Mrs. Penn said. Her voice sounded strange and tight, and her face was white under her tan. For a moment, I thought she might burst into tears.

Mrs. Tracey looked over at her, smiling, her eyes bright with excitement. I hated her! Who wanted to hear about a dead mother on a day like this?

"What a rotten subject to keep harping on!" my mother cried. It didn't take a genius to see that she was angry with Mrs. Tracey for insisting on talking about somebody who had died. "Come on, everybody, let's play softball. Kids, go get out of those swimsuits right now."

Jill came with me to the bathhouse, but Nancy stayed behind with her parents. The boys dressed and beat us back to the tables. Jill and I were laughing about our tangled hair when we returned with our wet swimsuits rolled up in our towels, and I didn't think to look around for Nancy.

Then Mom, Dad, Jill, and I started off toward

the baseball field. I saw my brother loping toward us with the ball and bat. Jill's brother and Luke followed us, talking about high school sports. Funny Uncle Duffy ran past us, whooping and leaping into the air like a lunatic, waving paper streamers and making everybody laugh. It was hard to believe that he was practically as old as Jill's mother.

I looked back. Chris and Rod were walking with the Standishes and Grandma, scuffing up dust on the dirt path with their feet. Suddenly they burst out laughing about something. Chris snapped a picture of Grandma. Behind them, his parents and Jill's strolled in a group, murmuring together.

But back at the tables, Mrs. Tracey and Maggie stood facing the Penns, and when I saw that, goose bumps prickled my skin. Nancy was still in her swimsuit, her arms clasped tightly over her chest as if she was cold. Her mother slipped her arm around her and hugged her close.

Mom had seen them, too. "If I ever get another idea like this picnic, I hope somebody locks me in the basement until I feel better," she said bitterly.

"Count on it," Dad said.

I ran toward the baseball field. "Come on, everybody, let's play ball!" I called out.

The day was still bright and sunny, but a shiver ran up my spine. I felt as cold as Nancy looked.

Chapter Five

We played ball for more than an hour in the hot sun, until almost five o'clock. By that time the park was crowded with people looking for places to sit and eat their dinners. Some of them had gathered up the things we'd left on our tables and put them on the grass, making room for their own picnic baskets. We were all a little embarrassed, and my parents and grandma apologized to the strangers.

"I think this is a signal that the party's over," Chris's father said, and my father agreed.

The grown-ups sorted out our belongings while the birthday kids stood to the side awkwardly, talking. Maggie and her mother were nowhere in sight—and neither were the Penns.

"Where's Nancy?" Jill asked, looking around.

"They must have gone home," Mom said, sounding dismayed. "Their picnic basket isn't here, and neither is the ice chest they brought."

"What do you think happened to Mrs. Tracey and what's-her-name?" Dad asked, scowling.

"I hope it was nothing trivial," Grandma answered.

Somebody laughed, then stopped. There was an embarrassing silence. Jill and I exchanged uneasy glances.

"I feel awful that we didn't say good-bye to the Penns," Mom said. "We hardly even got to know them. I should have made more of an effort."

"They were pretty quiet," Mrs. Corbett said. "They kept to themselves."

"I'm sure they were upset by all the talk about someone dying," Mrs. Standish said. "What a subject to bring up at a birthday party! I wish that Tracey woman had kept her big mouth shut."

"So do I!" Mrs. Corbett said. "And not just about the tragedy at the hospital. I never met anybody who bragged as much as she did. If she told me once about how much her car cost, she told me a dozen times." She stopped, blushed, and then laughed. "Sorry!" she said.

"Don't apologize," Grandma told her. "I enjoyed every word you said."

Everybody laughed then, even Mom, who hates it when people talk behind other people's backs.

We all started toward the parking lot at the same time. Behind the grown-ups, Chris walked with my brother and me, and Rod followed with Jill. I heard him ask her if she knew where Nancy lived.

Jill's Uncle Duffy, carrying an armload of stuff, walked with Nick, discussing baseball cards. It was hard to think of Duffy as a grown-up. I could see why Jill was so glad to have him for an uncle. I wondered again what the Traceys had said

38

about him that upset Jill so much that she ran away from the picnic. Maybe they thought he acted too much like a kid. Those Traceys!

Speak of the devils, I thought. There they were, Mrs. Tracey and Maggie, standing in the shade of a big maple near their car. They looked as if they were waiting for us. Oh, yuck, I thought, despairing. Now what?

"We thought we'd wait here to say good-bye to all of you," Mrs. Tracey said. "It's been an experience." Her laughter was as sharp as broken glass.

The grown-ups mumbled things like, "Goodbye, see you later," and "It's been wonderful," while they loaded picnic stuff into their cars.

Maggie grinned appreciatively at her mother. Then she looked at me and said, with the most sincere voice I'd ever heard, "Oh, Ceegee, you poor thing. You look terrible! That great big sunburned nose of yours could light up half of Seattle. Does it hurt?"

Gary sucked in his breath and looked as if he would explode. He teased me about my nose all the time, but even though he was the world's biggest brat, he still had enough brotherly loyalty not to side with Maggie and laugh at a remark like that. What she'd said was half sugar, half poison, and I couldn't stand it that I was letting her get away with it.

Maggie, pretending that she hadn't said anything rotten, smiled at Jill's brother and said, "Did you manage to have a good time today, Nick?" She was flirting with him, and implying that enjoying the picnic would have been close to impossible for a boy like him.

Nick raised his shades and stared at her for a moment, then said gruffly, "Not bad for kid stuff." I don't know if Maggie saw him roll his eyes or not, but I hoped so. After all, Duffy was his uncle, too, and whatever had upset Jill had probably upset Nick as well.

My ears were buzzing with humiliation. Had Chris heard what Maggie had said about my nose? Probably. Not that he hadn't already noticed it, of course.

My nose! My big, ugly, glowing nose! I could hire it out for a lighthouse. I hated it!

Dad had unlocked our car, so I piled into it. I could see Maggie talking to Jill about something, and Jill's face, which was as sunburned as mine, turned even redder. She stomped away from Maggie, toward her family's car.

Chris leaned in the open window next to me. "I'll send you prints of all the pictures I took," he said.

"Thanks," I muttered, sliding down into my seat. He seemed to be unaware of what was going on, but I was certain that he was only pretending.

"I had a great time," he said. "You're a good baseball player. A good swimmer, too."

"Thanks," I said again, turning my face away, hoping to hide the old beacon—as if that was actually possible.

"Well," he said slowly, "I guess I'd better go. I'm glad I met you and the others. Maybe we can

40

all get together again sometime. Next year for our birthdays. Or before."

I was dying inside. He was only being polite. Who wants to get together with somebody whose blazing nose could light up Seattle?

Rod came by to say good-bye. Then Uncle Duffy stuck his tousled head in the window and winked at me.

"Tell Jill good-bye for me," I said.

"You'll be hearing from her," he said.

One by one the cars left. Jill waved to me, but her smile was a little wobbly.

Maggie waved from her car, but I pretended I didn't see her.

"Did you have a good time?" Dad called back to me.

"Sure," I said. Then I realized that I didn't sound like somebody who'd been having fun. Mom had worked hard on this disastrous picnic. I was ashamed of my attitude.

"Yes, I had a good time," I said more enthusiastically. "It was a great picnic. Jill and Nancy are lots of fun. Chris and Rod were nice, too. But I wish I could have said good-bye to Nancy and her parents."

"I've got the Penns's phone number," Mom said. "You can call her when you get home. Maybe one of them wasn't feeling well. The sun was awfully hot."

"It was all that talk about somebody dying," Grandma said. "Mrs. Penn looked like she was going to faint or have a fit and sock somebody."

"Well, who'd blame her?" Mom said.

"Mom, do you remember anything about the woman who died?" I asked.

Mom shook her head. "No. I'm not even sure that anything like that happened. I'm not going to brood about it, though. I hope I never see Mrs. Tracey again."

From behind us in the van, Gary started laughing. "I wrote 'Ugly Cows' in the dust on the back of their car."

"Gary!" Mom shouted. "I told you before to stop doing things like that."

"Let him alone," Grandma said, grinning. "This is a land of free speech."

"Yeah," Gary said, satisfied. "They *were* ugly."

But they weren't. At least, not on the outside. Both Maggie and her mother were really gorgeous. I was the ugly one.

Macaw beak. Lighthouse nose. Was there a chance I was only exaggerating the problem? I fingered my nose. Nope. If anything, the problem was even bigger than I'd feared.

"Let your nose alone," Grandma said crossly. "It's fine. It's distinguished. You look like your aunt."

"She's got a big nose, too!" I cried.

Nobody understood how I felt. Nobody ever would.

After we got home, Mom gave me Nancy Penn's phone number. I called it three times, but no one answered.

I would have phoned Jill, but the call would have been long-distance. And maybe she didn't really want to talk to me or anybody else connected with the picnic. She'd been upset, too. Maybe she wasn't like me, wanting somebody to console her.

Maybe she thought I was ugly, too. She was too polite to make nasty remarks right to someone's face, though.

I looked at myself in the full-length mirror on my closet door for a long time that night. In a couple of weeks, I'd be starting seventh grade at a new school. I'd been teased about my nose before, in the early years at elementary school. What would it be like in a middle school, with strangers?

I was ugly, ugly, ugly. All of me. I was too skinny. My ribs showed. My elbows were the size of the knobs on my bedposts. I was knock-kneed. I had big hands and feet, so big they actually flapped. I was stuck with a gigantic horn for a nose. *Oogah, oogah.*

My hair was that terrible brown that everybody with common sense hated. It wasn't curly and it wasn't straight. It just hung there, looking *evil*.

Swamp-colored eyes. Nasty little green eyes so close together that they practically overlapped above my nose. You could find my eyelashes, maybe, if you looked for a long time with a magnifying glass.

How could I have lived for twelve years and never have noticed exactly how awful I really looked?

How could I start a new school now that I knew the truth about myself?

Maggie and her mother had destroyed me.

Chapter Six

Molly came back four days later, and I was so glad to see her that I practically bawled. I couldn't stand my own company any longer.

I'd spent the days after the picnic moping around the house and studying myself in mirrors, all mirrors. I'd even looked at my reflection in windows, on the chrome trim on the refrigerator, and on the smooth surface of the goldfish pond in the backyard. My nose seemed to be growing.

And peeling. By the time I started shedding my sunburn (like an ugly snake) I was certain my nose was at least an inch longer. Maybe even two.

But Molly made me feel lots better just by showing up on my porch one morning, holding a pottery cat she'd bought me in Mexico.

"Can we come in?" she asked.

I nearly knocked the cat out of her hands as I grabbed and hugged her.

"Happy birthday," she said. "I'm sorry I missed it. Did you have a party?"

"Don't even ask," I said. "It was too horrible to talk about." But I ended up telling her some of it, anyway.

"So what do the other girls say about it?" she asked when I finished. "I mean Nancy and—what was her name? Oh, yes, Jill. What do they say? Did they hate the picnic, too?"

"I haven't talked to them," I said. "Calling Jill would be long distance—oh, Mom said I could, but I haven't gotten around to it. And Nancy, well, she wasn't home the first few times I called and then I sorta forgot about it. You know how it goes. You get busy."

"Ha," Molly said. "You didn't forget about it. I know you. You were afraid she'd remind you of something that awful Maggie said and you'd start worrying about your nose again. It's been ages since you made such a fuss about it. How many times have I told you that it isn't half as big as you think it is? It's certainly not as big as your dad's—or your Aunt Cally's."

"Give it time," I groaned. "If it keeps on growing the way it has, I'll have to push it around in a wheelbarrow by the time I start high school."

Molly laughed. "That's dumb, Ceegee. Quit thinking about it. Just remember how much you'd hate weighing one million pounds, like I do."

Molly was only a little plump—just a tiny bit. But she had beautiful skin and all that glossy brown hair—and wonderful dark eyes—so I knew she was going to be the best-looking girl in middle school. But she didn't believe it.

Mom worked three days a week at the children's hospital as a lab technician, and she was rushing around getting ready to leave, but she stopped long enough to admire the pottery cat and compliment Molly on her tan.

"Be sure to help Grandma with the shopping," she told me. "And if you gave Snickers a bath this morning, I think I could see my way clear to paying for it."

"How much?" I asked suspiciously. Giving Snickers a bath was a terrible experience, but not for the usual reason bathing dogs was a problem. He didn't hate it. He loved it too much.

"Five bucks," Mom said.

"*I'll* wash him for that much!" Molly exclaimed, and then she said quickly, "Oh, no I won't. I remember what that crazy dog does."

"Don't dwell on it and it won't seem so awful," Mom said. "Molly, if you help, I can definitely see a fiver floating in your direction, too."

"Mother, for that much, you can take him to the Pampered Pooch for his bath," I argued.

"Not a chance," Mom said, on her way out the door. "The last time I took him there, they threatened to sue us or call the police or both."

She shut the door firmly, and Snickers, who understands English better than he ought to, trotted out of the kitchen, grinning.

"He heard," Molly said, despairing. "Why can't he be like our dog and not even know his own name?"

"You can go home if you want to," I said. "It will break my heart, but you can go."

46

"Let's make Gary wash the dog," Molly suggested.

"Are you crazy?" I exclaimed. "He's ten times worse than Snickers. Last time he gave the dog a bath, Mom had to call in the carpet cleaners."

"Gary washed the dog in the living room?" Molly asked, astonished. "I knew he was a pest, but . . ."

"No, no," I said. "That was where Snickers ran, after he rolled in the fertilizer Dad had brought home from the garden store. Gary forgot to shut the back door. And he left the hose running for hours."

Molly sighed. "Okay, why don't we get started then? I can use the money, and you can distract me by talking. I want to hear *all* the details of this picnic. Don't leave anything out."

"No way," I said, leading her—and Snickers—to the back door. "You tell me about California and Mexico. And don't *you* leave anything out."

Molly had lots of stories to tell, which was good, because it took nearly an hour to wash the dog. He tipped over the tub on the lawn the first time we filled it, because he got so excited that he jumped into it before we were ready. The next time he tipped it over because he was acting like such an idiot. Then, when we tried to rinse him off with the hose, he ran in circles, biting at the water and barking.

Grandma and Gary came out to watch. Grandma, who'd seen the whole mess enough times to know how to prepare, carried an open umbrella. Each time Snickers ran at her, prepared to leap up into the air and shake water on her, she held the umbrella in front of her.

After the dog's bath, Molly and I took turns showering in the little bathroom off the kitchen. Molly's shirt and shorts were too wet to put back on, so I gave her some of my clothes to wear home.

"I can barely squeeze into these," she groaned while she zipped up the shorts. "I can't believe how much fatter I got while we were on vacation. I must have eaten everything that wasn't permanently fastened to something else, and then developed amnesia."

"You didn't gain an ounce," I said. "Those shorts were always tight for me too."

"You lie but I love you for it," Molly said. We were in my bedroom, and she studied herself carefully in my dresser mirror. "Do you suppose I'll be called Fat Face Molly again this year?"

"No way," I said.

"Maybe if someone like that Maggie said something nasty to me, I'd get upset enough to stay on a diet."

I realized that I hadn't thought about Maggie Tracey since we began washing Snickers. "You don't need anybody like Maggie," I told Molly. "Trust me. She smiles at you and says things you can't get off your mind no matter how hard you try. She's like gum stuck to your shoe. Nightmare gum. Gum from outer space."

We went on to talk about school clothes, but my mind wasn't on anything but Maggie—and my nose. If I'd known before the picnic that she'd

48

be that nasty, I might have found a way to handle it. Maybe. I could have thought up lots of rotten things to say to her, and practiced them until I could rattle them off as if I acted like that all the time.

In a few more days, I'd be facing lots of new people. A whole school full of them. How many of them would make remarks about my nose? Or the rest of me? And how about my name? It was always good for laughs.

How come I didn't realize how hopeless I was until I turned twelve?

Maybe I was just plain stupid, too.

That evening I heard from Nancy Penn. I'd sorta pushed her out of my mind, the way I was trying to do with the whole memory of the picnic, so her phone call caught me off-guard.

"I've been meaning to get in touch with you," she said, "but something came up."

"You sound—well, I don't know. Unhappy or sad. Are you okay?"

"Sure," she said (I didn't believe her.) "The reason I'm calling is because Chris—remember him?—he called and said he had lots of prints of the snapshots he took at the picnic and he wanted to send a set to each of us. Or we could get together with Rod, he said, and have a sort of reunion, and he'd give us the pictures then."

I couldn't think of anything I'd hate more than a reunion, where we all sat around talking about that horrible party.

"I don't know," I said vaguely. "I'm pretty busy getting ready for school these days. And to tell you the truth, I'm not sure I want copies of the pictures Chris took. Who needs a couple dozen ugly snapshots of a nose like mine?" I tried to laugh, but I didn't carry it off very well.

"There's nothing wrong with your nose!" Nancy said, almost shouting. "You wouldn't say something like that if it hadn't been for that rotten Maggie! I never hated anybody so much in my whole life!"

"Then you can see why I'm not crazy to have prints of Chris's pictures," I said. "She'll be in a lot of them."

"We can throw those away!" Nancy declared. "The rest of the picnic was fun. And Chris is nice to offer us the prints, don't you think? Rod's nice, too. At the picnic, he said he'd be moving to my neighborhood this week."

"Then he'll go to your school," I said.

"I guess," she said. Suddenly she didn't sound very happy again.

"I thought you just said he was nice."

"He is, for a boy. But I'm not very enthusiastic about this reunion idea. Things got complicated." Her voice sounded strange, as if she was ready to cry.

"What's wrong?" I asked.

"Nothing. I'm tired of summer vacation, I guess. Well, if you're not interested in getting together—and I don't blame you—then I'll tell Chris to mail the pictures to you. Okay?"

"He doesn't even have to do that," I said. "Honestly. I don't want anything to remind me of the picnic. I liked meeting you and Nancy and your families. And the boys. But . . ."

"I know," Nancy said, sighing. "I know exactly what you mean. Well, that's all I wanted. I'll tell Chris not to bother sending you . . ."

"No, wait," I said. "That would hurt his feelings. I think there was enough meanness connected with the picnic. He can send them, and maybe I'll look at them some other time when I can look back and laugh. Like ten years from now."

Nancy laughed suddenly. "Good idea," she said. "I'll do the same."

"Well, maybe I'll call you sometime after school starts and I get used to things," I said finally, wanting to end the conversation as politely as I could. She was a nice girl. I didn't want to hurt her feelings, either.

"You bet," she said. "We'll keep in touch."

But after we hung up, I wasn't sure we would.

Molly and I went to a movie on the last Saturday afternoon before school started, which would have been great, except that we had to take Gary with us. I tried to make a bargain with him before we left—if he didn't talk, I'd buy him extra popcorn and ice cream at the theater. I should have told him that he wouldn't get the extra food until we were leaving, because he talked all the way through the movie anyway, no matter how many times Molly and I threatened to drag him outside and phone Mom.

We were on our way out of the lobby when I saw a girl with blond hair walking ahead of us.

She looked so much like Maggie that for a quick moment I had a big urge to turn around and run back inside the dark theater. It was only when the girl looked back over her shoulder at someone who was with her that I saw for certain that she wasn't Maggie. And even then my heart kept beating too hard.

This was stupid! Was I afraid of running into Maggie again?

Yes.

A few days later, Molly and I walked together for our first day in middle school. Neither of us could think of much to say. About a block from the school, she cleared her throat and croaked, "Maybe we'll have class with some of the kids from our sixth grade."

"Maybe," I said. I rubbed the tip of my nose. It felt red. Don't ask me what a red nose feels like. You'd know if it happened to you.

Molly sucked in her breath so that her stomach was flatter. "How do I look?"

"Fine," I said. "I'm telling the truth. I won't ask about me because I already know I look like a parrot."

"Stop that!" she said.

I shut up—but as soon as we walked in the main door of the school, I knew I was right. Two girls I'd never seen before stared at me. I thought I heard a boy laughing when I passed him. A teacher standing in a classroom door smiled pityingly at me.

If I only had beautiful hair like Molly, I thought, then maybe everybody wouldn't be staring at my nose. If only I had a closet full of expensive clothes. If only I was a genius or had some big, important talent.

If only I'd stayed home with my macaw beak. Down in the basement with the lights turned off and Snickers for company, because he loved me no matter what.

When we reached our first class, we did find a few kids from sixth grade there. We all smiled at each other and nobody looked particularly happy.

My nose and I sat down at a desk in back. Molly slipped into the seat next to me. Neither of us said another word.

After a while, a teacher strolled in and took roll. In my worry about my nose, I'd forgotten what a stupid name I had.

"Caledonia MacBride?" the teacher asked, looking around.

"Here," I said as I slid down in my seat.

She might just as well have called me Macaw MacBride, because half the class giggled while the other half looked at me with obvious pity.

Welcome to middle school. With any luck at all, I'd catch a fatal disease and be dead before I ever had to come back.

Chapter Seven

Middle school wasn't working out.

In every class, my silly name resulted in giggles. I dreaded roll call worse than a trip to the dentist. And even though nobody commented on my nose, it didn't take a genius to see that kids were laughing at it, also.

My clothes seemed all wrong, too, and I wasn't sure why. When Mom and I shopped for them during the weeks before school began, I'd thought that I'd picked great outfits. At least I'd believed that until the picnic. Somehow, afterward, I wasn't certain about anything anymore. I remembered Maggie—how good-looking she was, how sure of herself—and everything I wore seemed ugly or too young for me. Or the clothes made me look even skinnier.

Did Maggie ever look at herself in a department store dressing room mirror and hate what she saw? No way.

The last time Mom had taken me shopping, I'd

ended up in tears. We finally bought the skirt and vest I'd tried on, but I couldn't bring myself to wear them to school. They made me look bony enough to rattle when I walked, and my nose looked even longer.

Molly, who couldn't understand my problem at all, was having a slightly better time. But only slightly.

"If you were fat, you'd know how rotten really feels," she said one day in the school cafeteria. She poked her salad with her fork and sighed.

"You aren't fat and I do know how you feel, only worse," I said. The spaghetti I'd chosen was delicious. I considered going back to the food line for a second helping and decided that it wouldn't be tactful. Molly was trying hard to diet again. A true friend wouldn't pork out in front of her.

"Take a good long look at me," I said to her. "Notice the honker? It's long enough to hang over my upper lip now. Pretty soon I'll have to push it aside to eat."

Molly sputtered with laughter. "That's not true, Ceegee. If you're going to complain about how you look, do you have to be funny? I'm afraid of hurting your feelings when I laugh."

"Go ahead and laugh," I said. "That's what everybody else does. Here I am—Caledonia Macaw MacBride, owner of the world's largest and ugliest kazoo. I'm expecting the choir teacher to ask me to transfer to orchestra so I can play a horn solo. Just think—my folks won't even have to pay for the horn, either. I grew my own."

Molly screamed with laughter then, and the

kids sitting at the other end of the table grinned at us.

Oh, no! They heard me! I cringed inside. How stupid can you get, Ceegee? I asked myself.

Very stupid, was the answer.

But then I got a grip on myself. It wasn't as if they hadn't already noticed my nose, since it entered every room at least a half hour before I did.

I grinned back at them. "Awful, isn't it?" I asked.

"What is?" a girl with short, dark hair asked.

Molly nudged my ribs with her elbow. "She's talking about the spaghetti," she said.

"Hey!" I objected. "The spaghetti's great."

"But the chocolate pudding is disgusting," the girl said. "Don't ever get pudding here."

I nodded. "I'll remember that."

The girl got up and moved down the table to where Molly and I sat. She plopped down in the seat next to me.

"We have the same art class," she said. "And I'm in choir with you, too. But you never look up. I thought maybe you hated everybody."

I gawked at her. "Of course not!"

"Good," she said. "I'm Bernadette Singer, but don't call me Bernie. I hate that."

"Don't call me Caledonia," I said. "I hate *that.*"

"You're nicknamed Ceegee," Bernadette said. "I've heard kids talk to you in the hall." She nodded toward Molly and grinned. "Hey Molly. We've got math together."

Molly grinned back. "Sure, I remember you, Bernadette."

The three of us sat there for a long, awkward moment.

"Do you like this school?" Bernadette asked.

We shook our heads slowly.

"Do you suppose it gets better later on?" Bernadette asked seriously.

Molly sighed. "I hope so. We're stuck here for two years."

"Yeah," Bernadette said. "My brother went here. He said he liked it, but he lies about everything. I've never been so lonely in my whole life."

"But you've got those friends at the end of the table," I protested.

"I've known them since first grade," Bernadette said. "They don't count. We're all lonely and miserable. Except for you, nobody else has talked to us."

"That's how we feel," Molly said, and I nodded.

"But you started a conversation with us, so you can't be too shy," I told Bernadette.

"I heard you laughing," she said. "I figured you couldn't be awful if you hated the food."

Molly nudged me again, so I didn't volunteer the information that I'd been laughing at my nose.

"Art class is next," Bernadette said to me. "Maybe we could walk there together."

I nodded and shrugged, both at the same time.

"I've got typing next," Molly said. "I go in the opposite direction."

"Hey, Dina has typing next, too," Bernadette said. She waved at a pale blond girl sitting at the other end of the table. "Dina, this girl—Molly's her name—she's got typing next period."

Dina picked up her purse and notebook and joined us. "Did you see the pudding?" she asked Molly. "It looks so awful that I was afraid mine would explode and kill me."

"No, I bet it's the carrot cake that explodes and kills you," Bernadette interrupted, laughing.

"I thought the pudding looked wonderful," Molly said wistfully. "If I could have pudding, I wouldn't care if it blew up in my face."

"You're not dieting!" Dina exclaimed. "Don't do that! I dieted all summer, and I didn't lose one pound, but I was never so miserable in my whole life. Don't diet!"

She scuttled back to the other end of the table, took her pudding off her tray, and brought it back to Molly. "Here," she said. "I didn't touch it so it doesn't have germs in it. If you can stand the sight of it, eat it."

"Oh, yum!" Molly exclaimed, and she dug right in.

Bernadette grinned at me.

I felt a little better. Molly and I had made two friends. And nobody said a word about my nose. Or even my name.

But as Bernadette and I were leaving the cafeteria on our way to art, a boy we passed said, "Are you wearing a disguise or is that your real nose?"

Quick as a hornet, Bernadette flew over to him and batted his arm hard with her purse. "Pukey Parris, if you don't leave her alone, I'll tell her about the time in fourth grade when you threw up all over the globe during Parents' Night." She looked back at me. "He barfed all over the *world*, honestly. He really did. How's that for disgusting?"

The boy's face turned red, Bernadette laughed, and I marched out the door with a grin on my face.

But that was the end of the good times.

In art, Bernadette's table was across the room from mine, but she smiled at me, making me feel pretty good about myself, so I smiled at the boy next to me, whose name, I remembered, was Jack.

"Do you like this class?" he asked.

"Sure," I said. "Don't you?"

"I'd like it better if I could draw."

"This is where you're supposed to learn how," I said. "You're probably as good as anybody else in here."

"Maybe," Jack said, scowling, "but I doubt it."

Mrs. Crawford, the teacher, stood up in front of the class then and explained that in a few days we would start drawing people. Everybody groaned.

"It's not as hard as you think," she said. She darted to the chalkboard to show us how to place eyes and noses on faces.

"You'll learn that you haven't really been seeing people," she said. "Not really. You look but you don't *see*. And it's not only people that you're taking for granted."

She drew other things—cups and bowls, apples

and books, houses and trees—all from different angles.

By the time she finished explaining, I understood what she meant, and she was right. I had only been looking around me, but never *seeing*. Suddenly I was aware of the real shapes of objects. Why hadn't I ever noticed them before?

"We'll be drawing all sorts of things," Mrs. Crawford said. "But I'm anxious to begin using models. I'll need a boy and a girl to help out by posing for us."

Several girls raised their hands—the stuck-up girls. No boys volunteered, though. And naturally I slid down in my seat. No way would I let people draw pictures of me.

Mrs. Crawford smiled as she looked at the girls who had raised their hands. "Sorry," she said, "but I seldom take volunteers. I'm looking for certain kinds of faces, ones with prominent cheekbones and great profiles, and it's been my experience that ideal artists' models are usually too shy to think of themselves as subjects."

She glanced around the room, then pointed at a boy sitting near the windows. "Joe, you'd be perfect."

Joe Hiller turned red. "Hey, not me," he muttered.

But I could see why Mrs. Crawford picked him. He had strong cheekbones and a stubborn chin, and his mouth had a sort of curl to it, as if he was always smiling. He wasn't exactly good-looking—his face was too bony. But you'd notice him in a crowd, if you see what I mean.

I was still looking at him when Mrs. Crawford said, "And I believe the girl should be Caledonia. Notice how far apart her eyes are, what good cheekbones she has. And her mouth is nicely shaped. We'll pull her hair back to show off that beautiful hairline, too."

My ears were buzzing. I thought I was going to faint. Or simply drop dead. She was talking about me and everybody was staring at me. The girls who had volunteered weren't smiling, but everybody else was!

This was terrible. This was the worst thing that had ever happened to me. I'd been trying to hide my immense nose by letting my hair hang over my face, and here was a teacher talking about brushing back my hair to show my hairline! Was she crazy?

"By the way," Mrs. Crawford said to me, "I love your name. I suppose you know what Caledonia means—Celtic lass. It's my mother's name—her family are Scots. What's your middle name?"

"Uh, it's Giorsa," I mumbled. Everybody gawked.

"Do you know what that means?" Mrs. Crawford asked.

"Uh, it means grace."

"What does *my* name mean?" a girl named Diane asked.

Mrs. Crawford shrugged and laughed. "Gee, I didn't mean to get something started. I've got a book at home that tells about names, so I'll bring it tomorrow and all of you can look yourselves up."

The bad moment passed. Everybody was so interested in names that they forgot me and mine.

But my ears were still buzzing, and I wondered what I was going to do. Model for the art class? See my huge nose drawn over and over? Have the drawings show up all over school while kids laughed at me?

When class let out, Bernadette left with me. "You're sure lucky, being picked to model," she said.

"Are you crazy?" I exclaimed. "I can't! I won't! I couldn't stand having everybody stare at me for a whole period."

"But why?" Bernadette asked.

What was I supposed to say? That as the owner of the world's largest nose, I preferred to keep a low profile?

I told Molly about this disaster on the way home from school. She couldn't understand the problem, either.

"It's my nose," I said. "Please don't tell me that you can't see it. I was picked because of my huge nose. Nobody will have trouble drawing it."

"You're making this a lot worse than it is," Molly said. "It's not as if you were a freak, you know. The teacher wouldn't have picked you if there was actually something wrong with you. Some teachers are incredibly stupid, but none of them are that bad."

"I'll get sick and stay home from school that day," I said.

"She'll just wait for you to come back, I bet," Molly argued.

"Then I'll never go back!" I was practically bawling. Middle school was supposed to be fun, but I sure wasn't having any.

When I got home, Grandma was in the kitchen, helping Mom make noodles.

"Does this mean we're having homemade soup tonight?" I asked hopefully, distracted for a moment from my disaster.

"Yes, and I picked up some of that bread you like from the bakery," Mom said. "Did you happen to pass your brother on your way home?"

"Mom," I said patiently, "Gary and I don't go to the same school anymore. I come home from the opposite direction."

"That wouldn't stop Gary from ending up on your route," Mom said. "He has an appointment with the dentist this afternoon."

"Then he'll be late for sure," I predicted. I helped myself to a handful of crackers, fed one to Snickers, and sat on a stool. "You eating with us tonight, Grandma?"

"I make a point of never missing your mother's homemade soup," she said. She looked up at me curiously. "What's wrong? You look like somebody who's been tap dancing on the edge of a knife."

Mom looked at me then, too. "Your grandmother's right. What happened?"

I told them about art class.

"Wonderful," Mom said. "Maybe we can buy some of the drawings from the artists. I'd love to have sketches of you."

63

"Hey," I said, "you weren't listening. Mrs. Crawford asked me, owner of the world's most humongous nose, to model for the class. Nobody buys drawings of humongous noses unless they're on funny greeting cards."

"Your nose is fine," Grandma said briskly. "You look like Barbra Streisand. Or Cleopatra. Or that other Egyptian queen—what was her name?"

"Are you serious?" I cried. "I don't look anything like any other human being alive or dead. I look like an elephant! Or an anteater. Or a vacuum cleaner attachment."

At that moment, Gary strolled in the back door. "Am I too late to go to the dentist?" he asked innocently.

Grandma looked at her watch. "You're exactly on time, pal. Brush your teeth and hop in my car. I'm doing the honors today."

Gary slumped. "Oh, darn." He eyed me. "What's the matter?"

"Never mind," I said.

"She's going to model for her art class," Mom said.

"Mom!" I yelled.

Gary stared at me. "You're going to let them draw your nose?" he asked.

"Gary, brush your teeth or I'll brush them for you," Grandma shouted. "With a broom!"

Gary stomped off and I burst into tears. "See?" I cried. "My brother knows I'm ugly. I've got a nose like a macaw!"

Mom and Grandmother looked at each other.

"I'm hearing a long delayed echo from somebody at that birthday picnic," Mom said.

"No, you're hearing an echo from something in the back of a big, dark cave, something called Maggie," Grandma said. She sighed. "Ceegee, I wish I could give you amnesia. Or just wipe out bits of your memory. You weren't the only one who was hurt that day. Maggie and her mother did enough damage to last everybody a long time. But things are pretty sad when you'll let people like them tell you how to feel about yourself."

"You don't understand," I said.

"Sure I do," Grandma said. "I raised a daughter who looks very much like you. She was eighteen before she understood how attractive she was. Now she'll spend ten minutes trying to maneuver everybody around so that they see her in profile and she can show off those gorgeous earrings she collects and the fancy braids in her hair."

Aunt Cally was attractive. And different. But I wasn't. I was just plain, ugly Caledonia. And in a few days, I'd be plain, ugly, *desperate* Caledonia. The class sketches would be sold for Halloween decorations—or taped to my locker—or mailed to me in plain brown wrappers.

Molly phoned me after dinner, to talk about the book she was reading. I couldn't concentrate on what she was saying. The only thing I had on my mind was the art class.

Molly has been my friend so long that she can read my mind. "Are you still worrying about art?" she asked.

"Wouldn't you?"

"I would, because I'm so fat. But the teacher wouldn't have picked me for that reason. Nobody can see my bones. I'm like a bag of marshmallows."

Nothing she could say made me feel better. In the back of my mind, I could still hear Maggie's giggle. *Nose like a macaw. Nose like a macaw.*

At least Maggie hadn't made any remarks about my name. Then, of course, she hadn't been interested enough in me to ask why I went by a nickname instead.

Or maybe she thought my parents actually had named me Ceegee. I did sound like a fast-food restaurant, just like Dad said.

Darn it.

Chapter Eight

The weekend promised to give me a rest from misery. Two days without school, two days without the kids in art class staring at me, waiting eagerly for the chance to draw my nose.

Two days to think of something that would get me out of modeling for that class!

Molly came over for lunch on Saturday. We were eating on the back deck in the September sun when Dad came out and handed me a thick envelope.

"The mailman brought it for you," he said. "The return address says Chris Corbett. These must be prints of the pictures he took at the picnic." He looked as if he planned on standing around until I opened the envelope, so I went ahead and did it. He'd never have given me any peace otherwise.

He was right about the snapshots. The envelope contained a thick stack of them, wrapped in a brief note that said, "Here are the prints. I hope you like them. Give me a call and let me know what you think. Chris."

I handed the snapshots to Dad so he could look at them first. I didn't care if I ever saw them.

He went through them twice, saying over and over how good they were. Mom came out to see what was going on, and he gave them to her. She pronounced them the best snapshots she ever saw.

"Didn't Chris take great pictures, Ceegee?" she asked.

"Haven't seen them," I said.

"Here," she said, handing them to me. "Aren't they wonderful?"

The first picture showed Maggie, in her swimsuit, looking at least sixteen years old. In the background, Nancy and I were gawking at her. We looked really dumb. I tucked the picture under the stack quickly.

In the next picture, there I was. My nose actually cast a shadow! It did!

I handed the snapshots to Molly without looking at the rest. "You take them," I said. "I don't think my nerves can stand any more thrills."

"Ceegee, that's ridiculous," Dad said. "You look wonderful in all the pictures. You ought to have more self-confidence. You should . . ."

"Enough," Mom said briskly. "Let's let the girls decide if they like the pictures. Now come inside and give me a hand."

Dad followed her into the kitchen. We all do what Mom says when she uses that tone of voice.

Molly went through the stack quickly. "They're

good," she said. "You don't have to be scared to look." She held one snapshot close to her face. "Is the blonde with the nearly invisible bikini that Maggie you were talking about?"

"Yes," I said. "Can you believe she's only twelve?"

Molly sighed. "If I thought there was a chance I'd ever look like that, I'd give up eating entirely. I wouldn't even look at the labels on cans." She blinked and put the picture down. "I hate that girl. She's got the same kind of fake smile that I see every morning on the face of the girl who lockers next to me. You know what I mean? That smile that says she doesn't mind being nice to me as long as everybody around sees her doing it, it doesn't take much time, and she doesn't have to learn my name. Otherwise, look out."

"You see the problem," I said. "But you left out the worst part. Maggie smiled that way, sure, but she also said things—things that sorta sneaked up on me and stabbed me in the ribs before I knew what happened. She said she was very sorry that I had such a big nose. She told me that in front of other people! Then she giggled and said I was probably a very nice person anyway. Once she said she bet a million dollars I'd had to diet a lot, and that she was glad she never got fat because she didn't have even a speck of willpower."

"How come you didn't sock her?" Molly asked, and she sounded sincerely interested in my answer.

"I thought about it, but that would have spoiled the party."

"Some party," Molly grumbled. "You could have smashed your thumb with a hammer and had more fun."

"I know, but my mother went to a lot of trouble, calling everybody and planning things," I said. "I hope she never tries anything like that again, though."

Molly went through the rest of the snapshots and took out all the ones that had Maggie in them. "Why don't you toss these in the garbage?" she said. "That way, you'll be able to look through them and remember the good parts of the picnic."

That was such a great idea that I jumped up and took the Maggie pictures straight to the garbage can.

"Eat dirt and die," I said to the pictures as I dropped them in the can.

On the deck, Molly laughed. "Now that's more like the Ceegee I know."

I showed the pictures to Grandma later in the day, after Molly left. Grandma went through them slowly, smiling. But when she finished, she looked up at me and said, "How come there aren't any of Her Royal Pain and the Queen Mother?"

"I threw them out," I said.

"Good for you," Grandma said. "I've tossed out a few snapshots in my time, too. No point in being sentimental about a snake bite."

Grandma could cheer up anybody.

*　　*　　*

I found myself eating more at meals—not that I'd ever passed up any second helpings. But Maggie's remark about how I looked like I dieted made me more aware of how skinny I was.

Maggie, Maggie Maggie! I'd known her only a few hours and yet, somehow, I managed to spend a lot of time every day going over and over things she'd said and the looks she'd given me.

In a way, I was doing all this to myself. But how could I stop?

Tell yourself she was only a stranger you saw once, I thought, and so who cares what she said about anything? But that didn't work.

I wandered into Grandma's apartment the next afternoon. She was cutting warm coffee cake, and when she saw me, she slid an extra large piece on a plate and handed it to me.

"Why so gloomy?" she asked. "Is it school?"

"It's everything," I said.

"I remember feeling like that when I was your age," she said. She poured coffee for herself and gestured to me to sit down at her breakfast bar. "I wish I could tell you that you'll feel lots better next year. But how we feel pretty much depends on how we decide we're going to feel—if you see what I mean."

"You're saying that I make up my own mind about how I'll feel," I said. The cake was delicious and I practically forgot Maggie for a moment or two.

"You're still embarrassed about that birthday picnic," Grandma said. "I can see why. It hurts to hear yourself talked about in front of strangers. But don't you see that the Traceys intended for you to feel like that? You're letting them get away with it."

"Maybe," I said. "It's hard to believe that people do things like that on purpose. I figured that they just blabbed out loud the stuff that the rest of us only think."

"There are no accidents," Grandma said. "People say what they intend saying. If you start making excuses for them, it gets easier and easier for them to act like slobs. And in the long run, you're the one who gets hurt. They were really rude and stupid. Now put all their meanness out of your mind. You wouldn't care if the garbage man said something rude to you, would you?"

I couldn't help but laugh. "As a matter of fact, he did," I told her. "One day last spring, when it was raining hard, he told me that Snickers and I looked like we were related. Two skinny, wet mutts."

Grandma looked up at me sharply. "He did? John Jefferson dared say that to you? I'll make a point of talking to him about that the next time he comes."

"Don't, Grandma," I said, laughing. "I got even. I told him he must be an expert on skinny, wet mutts, because people were always asking me if Snickers was his brother."

Grandma grinned slyly. "I'd say you're a chip off the old block, but your father could never have come up with that. I guess the sass skipped a generation. Good for you. Now apply that same spirit to your memories of that picnic."

Oh, Grandma, I thought, I keep trying, but it doesn't work.

I'd spent most of Sunday worrying about Monday, which doesn't make a lot of sense unless you've had problems as bad as mine. I wasn't looking forward to art class and I still hadn't thought up an excuse that would get me out of posing without admitting that I thought I was too ugly for the job.

Sunday night, I studied myself in the triple mirror in the downstairs bathroom. The longer I looked, the longer my nose got. I experimented with some of Mom's makeup, but that seemed to make things worse. I tried a couple of new hairstyles. Hopeless. I draped a towel over my head, leaving a tiny opening I could peer out of. Perfect. But I knew I couldn't get away with wearing it to school.

Monday came, along with a terrible rainstorm that required both raincoats and umbrellas for Molly and me. We slopped to school, splashing in puddles, talking about what we'd do if we inherited a million dollars from some old uncle we never heard of (so we wouldn't have to feel bad that he was dead).

"I'd leave today for a place where rain never falls," Molly said.

"I'd go someplace where enormous, ugly noses were in fashion," I said. "I wouldn't care whether it rained or not."

"You're exaggerating again," Molly said.

"No, I'm not!" I cried, and I stamped extra hard in a puddle. "You have a tiny nose so you don't know what I go through. I need to have plastic surgery. I begged my parents before to let me have the end of my nose cut off, but they said I was too young and my nose wasn't that bad and someday I'd be glad I looked like the rest of my family. Can you believe that?"

"Sure," Molly said. "It makes lots of sense. What doesn't make any sense is the idea you have that your nose is growing."

I felt the tip of my nose. "Okay, maybe it isn't growing an inch a day. Not quite. But you have to admit that nobody like me has ever posed for an art class before."

"The only thing I know is that nearly every girl in this school would have loved being chosen to model for the class," Molly said stubbornly. "You're the one who was picked. You're making too big a deal out of this, Ceegee."

I gave up. There was no way I could ever make Molly understand. And she was my best friend, too.

School days are usually very long. This one wasn't. It seemed that I hardly shoved my raincoat in my locker before it was time for art.

And maybe this was going to be the day I had to model!

It wasn't. As soon as I reached class, I asked Mrs. Crawford and she said, "No, later in the week."

"When?" I asked. I was having such a horrible

anxiety attack that my toes had tied themselves into knots.

"In a day or two," she said. "I need to show the class a few things first."

But she didn't get much done that day, because she'd brought the book that told the meanings of different names. Nobody wanted to do anything but look through it, so I sat at my desk, miserable enough to wish I'd stayed home in bed with the cold I had hoped to come down with the day before.

"What's the matter?" Bernadette asked after she'd had her turn with the book.

"Not much," I said. "Except that if I have to look stupid, I wish I could have done it today and gotten it over with. I hate suspense."

Bernadette stared at me. "Do you realize that I don't have any idea what you're talking about?"

"Modeling," I said. "Remember? I have to model for this class. I was wishing that I could have done it today and then I wouldn't have to worry anymore about the end of the world because it would already be here."

"The end of the world is not coming because this class makes sketches of you," she said. "Think how jealous some of the girls will be. They wanted to do it, and the teacher picked you instead."

"Yeah," I said miserably. "Lucky old me."

Most of the class was over when Mrs. Crawford finally put the book away. She drew a big oval on the chalkboard, then stuck a couple of eyes and a smiling mouth on it.

"This is not a portrait," she said.

Next to that oval, she drew another, but this time she didn't put in the eyes and mouth. Instead, her chalk flew over the new oval, quickly sketching out straight and curved lines, some of which crossed each other.

"Here are the average proportions of most faces," she said. "See? Usually eyes are set about here. Notice how the top of the ear lines up with the eyebrow? See where the lower part of the nose comes?"

I touched the place where my nose ended. It seemed to be about where she had drawn a line on the oval on the chalkboard!

Why did I look so weird, then? Because my nose stuck out so far in front? I wanted to go home so I could look at my face in the triple mirror again.

No, I didn't. I wanted to be queen of the entire world so that I could declare mirrors illegal.

I bent my head, hiding behind the curtain of my hair. The year before, in sixth grade, I hadn't cared too much how I looked. Not too much. I seldom worried about my nose, unless somebody had been teasing me. There seemed to be more important things to think about. Maybe I had believed that I looked practically as good as any of the other girls in my class. I was such a kid.

But something had gone wrong at the picnic. A perfect stranger had managed to make me feel awful about how I looked. And then I started noticing, *really* noticing my face. And even my big feet. And my swamp-green eyes. And my plain, ordinary hair.

When I was a little girl, my favorite fairy tale had been "The Ugly Duckling." I pestered Mom to read it over and over to me until I learned to read it myself. I even read it to Snickers.

Now I hated that story, because some of us ugly ducklings were never going to grow up into swans.

Chapter Nine

Chris phoned me that evening, which surprised me. "How'd you like the snapshots?" he asked.

"They were great," I said. My face burned when I remembered that I'd thrown some of them away, the ones with Maggie in them. "I was going to write you a thank-you note."

"That's okay," he said. "Do you want another set? Or just copies of a few of the pictures? Rod's grandmother couldn't come to the picnic, so she wanted her own set."

"My parents liked the picture that has our whole family in it, so they're going to have it enlarged," I told him. "They said you're a good photographer. I think so, too."

"Thanks," he said. "But I'm not sure everybody agrees with you. I called Nancy to see if she wanted more, but she didn't sound very happy about the idea. I don't think she liked them much."

"Maybe she didn't have a good time at the picnic," I said. There was no *maybe* about it, I thought. I knew she hadn't enjoyed herself. Apparently only the boys managed to avoid trouble with Maggie. "But," I went on quickly before he took my remark personally, "I'm sure she liked the pictures you took."

"I hope she did," he said, sounding unconvinced.

"What did Maggie say about them?" I asked. My heart skipped a beat and my mouth felt dry.

"Maggie?" Chris asked, as if he'd never heard the name before. "Maggie? Gee, I guess I forgot to send anything to her."

I didn't believe him. And I was grinning such a big grin that my face felt as if it was going to split in half. I was glad that Maggie didn't have the pictures, and I was sure she'd want them—to gloat over.

"It's probably too late now to send a set to her," I told Chris. "After all, it's been a long time since the picnic. Days and days and days."

"Weeks, almost," he said. "September will be over before we know it, and she certainly wouldn't be interested in summer snapshots then."

I could hear laughter in his voice. Chris wasn't half bad for a boy. You could be friends with him.

"How do you like middle school?" I asked.

"Hey, it's great," he said. "There's a camera club, and a great band—I play the clarinet. And I don't have to take the bus because the school's only a few blocks away. Last year I had to ride miles on the bus."

"I can walk to my middle school, too," I said. "I wish it was on the other side of the earth, though. It's a rotten school."

79

"Why?" Chris asked. "What's wrong with it?"

"Nobody's very friendly," I said. "And there are too many kids. It's at least three times as big as my elementary school. And the teachers are crabby." Except for Mrs. Crawford, I added to myself. In spite of that modeling problem, she was nice.

"Maybe you'll get used to it," Chris said.

"Sure," I said, but only because he was so cheerful.

After he hung up, I got out the pictures he'd taken and looked through them again. I noticed for the first time that Nancy was never smiling. My smile was fake a lot of the time, but she hadn't even tried.

On impulse, I called her up. I hadn't planned on getting involved with any of the birthday kids, but Chris had called me—and then I looked at the pictures again and saw how unhappy Nancy looked. Heck, I thought, why not call and see how she's getting along?

She sounded unhappy on the phone, too.

"What's new with you?" I asked. "How do you like your school?"

"Okay, I guess," she said, her voice quiet and glum.

"Are you making lots of new friends?" I asked.

She was silent for a moment, and then she said, "A few. But I'm pretty busy with other things."

"Do you see Rod Standish around school?"

"Not often," she said.

I told her that Chris had called to find out if I wanted more prints of his pictures. "I said that

80

I didn't, and I hope I didn't hurt his feelings," I told her. "But honestly, I don't need anything to remind me about that picnic."

"It was pretty awful," Nancy said. "I wish I hadn't gone."

"Because of what Maggie said about your clothes?" I asked. "You looked a lot better than I did. And I didn't think *she* looked so great. If her clothes had been any tighter, they'd have split at the seams."

"Maybe they were left over from fifth grade," Nancy said, and suddenly we both began laughing.

"Right, maybe that was the problem," I said. "I could send her some of my stuff. It would fit her better."

"We could make up a box of clothes for her," Nancy said, gasping for breath between giggles. "And another for her mother."

"We could throw in a book on manners," I said. "My grandmother's got one—sometimes she reads aloud from it to my brother, Gary."

"Does it do any good?" Nancy asked. "I seem to remember that your brother is—well, stubborn."

"You noticed that he's a brat?" I asked frankly. "Actually, he's disgusting. He eats sandwiches made out of mayonnaise and raisins for breakfast."

"Oh, ugh!" Nancy cried. "He really is disgusting."

"We could send him to Maggie," I said.

"Are you sure he deserves something that awful?"

I pretended to think for a moment or two. "We

couldn't send him by himself," I said finally. "We'd have to send the dog with him for company."

Nancy was shouting with laughter, and I was glad I cheered her up. "I wish you went to my school," I said sincerely.

"So do I," she said, and she sounded just as sincere. "What are your teachers like?"

"Well, not all that great. There's one who's nice—Mrs. Crawford, the art teacher." And then, because I was feeling so comfortable with Nancy, I told her about how Mrs. Crawford wanted me to model for the class.

"You ought to be glad," Nancy said. "Gee, nobody ever asked me to do anything like that."

"Think about what I look like," I said. "If you've forgotten already, take out the pictures. And remember, I'm the one the hospital nurses said looked like a macaw."

"I didn't believe that dumb story!" Nancy shouted. "Maggie's rotten mother made it up. Your nose doesn't look anything like a parrot's. Not anything at all!"

"But would you pose for an art class if you looked like me?" I asked. "Honestly, now. Would you?"

"Yes, yes, yes!" Nancy cried. "I'd love it. And so will you. Listen, quit thinking about what Maggie and her mother said. They are the worst people in Seattle. They ought to be run out of town. Every time I remember them, I get so mad I could call them up and tell them exactly how mean and stupid and ugly they are."

"I know how you feel," I said. "I lie awake at night imagining doing things like that."

"It's like they put some sort of curse on us," Nancy said.

"I know my nose has grown longer since the picnic," I said. "I'm sure it has. It's because I think about it so much."

"Well, I certainly don't believe *that,*" Nancy said. "You can't think about something and make it grow. If that was possible, then I'd give myself longer eyelashes."

"I'm glad I called you," I blurted. "I was feeling awful, but talking to you has made me feel lots better."

"So you'll model for the art class, right?" Nancy said.

"I didn't say that!" I cried. "This conversation hasn't changed how I look. I can't model!"

"Do it," Nancy said. "I bet nobody ever asked Maggie to model for anything. Do it, and then see if one of the kids will give you a drawing. You can send it to Maggie. Wouldn't that make her mad?"

"No, she'd laugh herself sick," I said bitterly. "One look at the famous MacBride nose, and she'll know she didn't dream it up after all."

"You're starting to feel bad again," Nancy said. "Don't. We can't let her win this way. The only reason she came to the picnic was to make as many people miserable as possible. We've got to stop this."

"How?" I asked. "If I knew how to forget her, don't you think I would?"

Nancy sighed. "I guess you're right. It's not that easy."

Mom interrupted me then, saying she had to

use the phone, so I told Nancy I'd call her again sometime and I hung up.

I went to the triple mirror and studied my face carefully. And I sighed. No matter how hard I tried, I couldn't see myself any other way than the way I really was. Ugly.

At school, Bernadette and her friend Dina had lunch with Molly and me every day. We found out that they lived near the Metro line, and so it wouldn't be too hard to get together after school or on Saturday.

"Bernadette lives in a great old house," Dina told us. "You can see clear across Lake Washington from her bedroom window."

Bernadette nodded while she swallowed the last bite of her sandwich. "I've got a view of Sandy Beach. In winter, it's dismal. But in the summer, it's nice."

I shuddered a little. I didn't like hearing anything about Sandy Beach anymore.

In the next art class, Mrs. Crawford practically scared me into a coma by asking Joe to sit on a stool in front of the class so that we could draw him. I was afraid that I had only a few minutes before she'd call me up next. I was so nervous that I couldn't draw Joe, no matter how hard I tried. And I forgot everything Mrs. Crawford had taught us about where eyes go. I ended up drawing a face that looked much more like a cat's than a boy's.

Every minute or so I checked my watch against the clock on the wall. For a while I thought both of them had stopped. It was the longest class I'd ever lived through.

Rain began falling suddenly, splashing against the windows. Autumn wasn't here yet. We'd have a month of fairly good weather before the serious winter rains began. But summer was over. Every morning on the way to school, I smelled autumn in the air.

Next summer, I told myself, my family will go to Sandy Beach again, and I won't even remember Maggie or that awful birthday picnic. In fact, I won't remember her or the things she said by the middle of next week.

I was determined to do a better job on my sketch, so I erased half the lines on my paper and tried harder to draw Joe. But nothing helped. Not only was I a rotten artist, but I was also so scared that my hand shook.

Finally, unbelievably, the bell rang and the class was over. I hadn't been called to model! I bolted toward the door without waiting for Bernadette. Safe! Maybe Mrs. Crawford had changed her mind.

But as I passed her desk, she called out, "Wait, Ceegee. I want to talk to you."

I didn't have a choice. I stopped.

"Do you have a pair of big hoop earrings?" she asked. She made a circle with her finger and thumb to show me how big she meant.

I shook my head. "I don't, but my grandmother does. Why?"

"Could you borrow them for tomorrow?"

I gaped at her. "What for?" I asked.

"Tomorrow's the day you sit for us," she said. "I'd like you to wear big, dramatic earrings. If you can't get your grandmother's, then I'll bring mine for you."

My tongue stuck to the roof of my mouth and I was afraid that it was never coming loose.

Mrs. Crawford turned away to talk to someone else then. Hadn't she noticed that I was completely paralyzed? My parents would need to come to school and carry me home on their shoulders like a board.

"Come on, Ceegee," Bernadette said. She nudged me.

I came back to life. My tongue unstuck from the roof of my mouth. I swallowed. My feet marched automatically toward the door.

"You okay?" Bernadette asked. "You look weird."

"That's because I *am* weird," I said. "And I look weird. And tomorrow I have to sit in front of the whole class so you can all laugh at me. And I'll be wearing my grandmother's earrings, too."

"Are they awful?" Bernadette asked. "Why wear them if they're awful?"

"They're gorgeous," I said. "But with a big, round earring on each side of my face, my nose is going to look like one of those old cannons in the park. You know, the ones on wheels."

All the way to our next class, Bernadette screamed with laughter.

Chapter Ten

As soon as I got home, I borrowed Grandma's earrings. Then Molly and I locked ourselves in my bedroom and I tried them on in front of my mirror.

I was right. With my long snout bracketed by two big gold circles, I did look like a cannon. "If I sneeze tomorrow, everybody in the room will think a war has broken out and they'll crawl under their tables," I said.

"You are being ridiculous!" Molly insisted. "You look great. I love those earrings. The art class will be crazy about you—wait and see."

Outside the door, my rotten brother yelled, "Open up, Ceegee. Let Snickers in! You closed your door in his face and hurt his feelings."

Gary didn't care whether or not the dog was shut out of my bedroom. He wanted to know what was going on.

I unlocked my door and yanked it open. Snickers wasn't even in the hall.

"You're wearing Grandma's best earrings!" Gary yelled. "Does she know you have them? Boy, are you going to get in trouble if you took them without asking. I'm going to tell."

I slammed the door.

"Could you possibly take Gary home with you?" I asked Molly. "Don't you need a brother?"

"I wouldn't mind having one," she said, "but Gary is definitely not the one I want. Forget him and let's do things with your hair."

I sat on the bed while she brushed my hair into different styles. "Anything looks good on you," she said generously, but I didn't believe her.

"You have to say that because you're my friend," I grumbled. "Tell me the awful truth. What do I look like with my hair brushed straight back? Mrs. Crawford wants me to wear it like that so my hairline will show."

Molly brushed and I kept my eyes shut until she told me to look.

There my nose was, all over my face. Without the veil of hair, there was nothing else to look at but my nose. And the earrings.

I clawed my hair back in place. "I am definitely coming down with a fatal disease before tomorrow morning," I told Molly as I removed Grandma's earrings. "Or I'm leaving town. But I'm absolutely not sitting in front of that class with my nose hanging out."

"Yes, you are," Molly said. "A year ago you would have done it. You'd have been calling me up day and night to talk about it. You let that nasty girl at the picnic change you—and wouldn't she be glad if she knew!"

"Well, I'm not going to give her the satisfaction by phoning her and telling her that she's ruined my life," I said.

"You might as well," Molly said. "If you ever see her again, she'll know in a second that she hurt you."

"Oh, thanks!" I cried crossly. "I hope I'm a better actress than that!"

"Are you?" Molly asked. "Then prove to me how good you are. Walk into that class tomorrow as if you could hardly wait to model for the kids. Pretend it until it comes true."

I stared at her for a long moment. "Okay, I'll do it. As soon as you go clothes shopping with me and pretend that you're having a good time when the skirt you try on won't zip up."

"Ceegee!" Molly protested angrily. "That's not fair!"

I shrugged. "It's as fair as pretending that I'll be glad to sit in front of a room full of people who are practically strangers and let them draw ugly pictures of me."

Molly was about to argue, but Gary came back and pounded on my door again.

"Mama says that if Molly's staying for dinner, does she want a baked potato or rice?" he shouted.

Molly yanked open the door. "Both!" she cried.

Gary ran off as if we were chasing him.

"I shouldn't have told him that," Molly said.

"He'll never let me forget it. Anyway, I haven't asked my mother yet if it's okay."

"Call her," I said. "I need to have you around tonight."

But Molly's mother wanted her to come home quick, because her aunt and uncle from Canada had just arrived for a surprise visit, so I was left by myself, in front of my bedroom mirror.

I brushed back my hair and put the earrings on again.

"Mirror, mirror," I said, "who is fairest in the land?"

"Maggie Tracey," I answered myself. And I grabbed up a scarf and draped it over my whole head so I couldn't see.

Snickers barked once from the open doorway, but when I pulled back the scarf to look at him, he'd disappeared. Probably not even dogs want to hang around with crazy people.

At breakfast the next morning, I hoped that no one would remember that I was fated to make an idiot of myself that afternoon. I didn't feel I could bear to begin the day by talking about the problem.

Grandma had shuffled in just as Mom was pouring juice, to tell us that she'd fixed French toast for herself and couldn't understand why, since she hated it and always had.

"I seem to remember that you make awful French toast," Dad said. He was reading the classified ads in the morning paper while eating toast and canned peaches. "Say, someone is selling a hundred-year-old rug. That's pretty old. What do you suppose it looks like?"

"Not like anything we'd be interested in," Mom said automatically. She invited Grandma to sit down and have breakfast with us.

Grandma looked at Gary, who was adding cornflakes to the mayonnaise and raisins on his white bread. "I don't have to sit by him, do I?" she asked.

"Ceegee and her nose are posing for her art class today," Gary said, without looking up.

I considered stabbing him with my spoon, but it probably wouldn't have hurt enough. "Sit by me, Grandma," I said. "Don't talk to Gary."

"Here's another interesting ad," Dad said to nobody in particular. "Somebody is selling used bus windows."

"Don't you care that your daughter is modeling for her art class today?" Grandma asked Dad.

Dad lowered the paper. "I thought that it would be tactful not to talk about it, especially since my son and heir has already laid the groundwork for a battle." But he smiled at me. "You're going to do just fine, Caledonia Mac-Bride," he told me. "I'm not worried about you."

"I hope the earrings work out," Grandma said.

"They're beautiful," I said. I gulped down the last of my orange juice. "Maybe I can ask the teacher if the class can draw them without me attached to them."

"Good idea," Gary said.

"Gary, if you don't quit that, I'm going to ask

your grandmother to read another chapter in the manners book to you," Mom said.

"Read the chapter on escorting young ladies to dances," I suggested. I'd seen the book. Nothing in it could help Gary.

"Oh, barf!" Gary yelled. "I'm never going to escort anybody anyplace."

"You're right about that," I said. "Nobody wants to go anywhere with you."

"Oh, lord," Dad breathed. He folded the paper and stood up. "I've got to leave now. Daughter, stop worrying. Son, *start* worrying. Mother, don't feed that French toast to the dog because he's getting fat. Wife, I'll be home at the usual time."

"Well, that was short and to the point," Grandma observed as Dad left. "He's beginning to sound like the classifieds."

Molly came in the back door a second after Dad walked out. "Ready for the big day?" she asked me.

"No, but I don't have a choice since I woke up alive instead of dead this morning," I said. "So much for wishing on stars." I grabbed my jacket and book bag.

"Got the earrings?" Molly asked.

I patted my book bag. "Right here. Maybe I could bring that coil of rope in the garage. Then I could hang myself in class and make a really interesting subject for the sketches."

"Wouldn't work," Gary said as he spread mayonnaise on a second sandwich. "The loop wouldn't fit over your . . ."

"Gary!" Mom and Grandma yelled.

I slammed the door behind Molly and me. "I don't know how I go on living here without losing my mind," I said as we hurried down the steps. "Did you ever notice that my family isn't normal?"

"Who has a normal family?" Molly grumbled. "When I left, both my parents were crawling around on the bathroom floor looking for a little piece of plastic that broke off my father's retainer."

"Your father wears a retainer?" I asked.

"He waited until he was forty to have his teeth straightened. Can you believe it? And he's always breaking things. I can't remember how many times he had to have his braces repaired. Mother's different. She never breaks anything, she just loses it all—keys, purses, books, clothes. Once I found one of her contact lenses floating in a paper cup on the kitchen counter. I practically drank out of that cup!"

"At least you don't have Gary," I said.

"Yeah," she said, sounding so thankful that I was embarrassed.

I can't remember what school was like that morning. I think I was in a coma. By the time art class came around, my knees were knocking together. Bernadette kept up a steady mutter in my ear—don't be scared, don't panic, it'll be fine, you look wonderful, talk talk talk.

"Hush," I whispered to her as we passed Mrs. Crawford's desk. "You aren't helping."

"Today's the day, Ceegee," Mrs. Crawford said. "Did you remember the earrings?"

I nodded and scurried toward my seat.

"Just leave your things on your table," Mrs. Crawford said. "You'll be sitting right here." She patted the stool that stood in front of the class. My stomach turned over and settled in my shoes.

I approached her slowly, holding the earrings in one sweaty hand. Kids were taking their places around the room. Somebody giggled, and I knew it was at the sight of me, fastening on the earrings.

Mrs. Crawford produced a brush and pulled back my hair. Then she took out a long, striped scarf and wrapped it around my head, tucking the ends under. I could only imagine what I must have looked like by then. It was a miracle that nobody screamed or threw up.

"Now," Mrs. Crawford said, sounding pleased for some reason. Teachers can be so strange sometimes. "Sit a little sideways, Ceegee, so that the light from the window strikes one side of your face. Raise your chin. Lean forward just a bit. Perfect."

There was a weird clanging in my head. My knees went right on knocking. I heard the whisper of paper, the scratch of pencils, a low murmur from the back of the class.

"Notice how the left side of Ceegee's face is shadowed," Mrs. Crawford said. "See how the shadow has almost the same value as her hair. The scarf makes a nice, dramatic contrast."

I realized for the first time that Mrs. Crawford was sketching, too. I turned my eyes to look.

"No, Ceegee, look at the back of the room," she

said quickly. "And you've changed position. Move forward."

Posing was hard work. Not only was my stomach on fire, but my back was, too. And my legs ached. Around the time I thought I'd been sitting there for half an hour, Mrs. Crawford told the class it was time for my first rest break.

"Stand up and move around, Ceegee," she told me.

I got to my feet stiffly and gaped at the wall clock. Only ten minutes had passed. Unbelievable. I had to model for years and years more! This class was never going to end.

I saw Bernadette grinning at me. Several of the other kids were smiling, too. But some were bent over their drawings, correcting lines or erasing.

Mrs. Crawford told me to sit on the stool again, and I did, assuming the same position I'd held before. This time it seemed easier. My knees quit knocking.

Since I wasn't so uncomfortable now, I had time to worry. How many people were drawing my nose right at this very moment? I thought. Did I hear somebody laughing? Were they all smirking at me?

Another break. I tried to sneak a look at Mrs. Crawford's sketch, but she turned it so I couldn't see it. Bernadette didn't look up at all. Instead, she was scowling down at her paper.

Now she knows what I was talking about, I thought. Now she has to admit that I'm ugly.

Finally Mrs. Crawford told the class that time

was up. I tried to act casual, as if I didn't really care one way or another about that whole awful ordeal. I took off Mrs. Crawford's scarf, folded it, and put it on her desk before I returned to my table. Without looking around, I removed Grandma's earrings and put them in my bag.

The girl who sat in front of me turned around. "You're a good model," she said. "You hardly moved at all. Look." She held up her drawing.

"Who's that?" I blurted stupidly.

"You," she said.

I recognized the earrings, but that was all. The girl she'd drawn looked more like her than me.

"Not bad," the boy next to her said as he examined her sketch. He showed me his. He wasn't much of an artist. I didn't even recognize the earrings. "I know it's pretty bad," he said. "All I can draw are trees."

"I can tell," I said, and then I laughed a little. The girl he'd drawn didn't resemble a tree, exactly, but her neck was almost long enough.

When the class was over, I bolted to the door, but Mrs. Crawford stopped me.

"Nice job," she said. "I had a hunch you'd be good." Then she handed me her sketch. "Here, you take this so you'll have something to help you remember today."

I looked down at her drawing. Behind me, Bernadette said, "Wow."

Mrs. Crawford had made me seem mysterious and—glamorous! The earrings and the scarf didn't look stupid on me. They looked great. Different, but great. My eyes seemed bigger because my hair was pulled back.

And my nose—well, it certainly wasn't an ordinary nose. But in Mrs. Crawford's sketch, it did look like the sort of nose an Egyptian queen might have had a long time ago. Suddenly I was sorry that I'd taken off Grandma's earrings.

And just as suddenly I understood why Aunt Cally wore her hair pulled back and owned more pairs of wild earrings than anybody else I knew. She was different-looking, but she was gorgeous. Exotic, like some sort of wonderful, foreign flower.

I looked at Mrs. Crawford and felt a blush spread up my neck to my forehead.

"So you finally figured it out," she said, and she laughed. "You're unconventionally beautiful, Ceegee. And you'll look more beautiful every year of your life. Lucky you."

Molly and I ran home from school that day. Grandma was in the kitchen with Mom when we burst in. I took Mrs. Crawford's sketch out of my bag and held it up.

"Look at me," I said. I couldn't quit smiling.

Grandma and Mom studied the sketch for a long time. "Wonderful," they both kept saying. "Beautiful."

Mom took a long look at me. "I like your hair pulled back that way," she said. "You look older—well, a little older, anyway."

I got Grandma's earrings out of my bag and held them up to my ears. "Nice, huh?"

"Perfect," Grandma said. "They look better on you than they do on me, so you keep them."

"Oh, she can't," Mom said. "They're too expensive."

"They're hers," Grandma said. She took another long look at the sketch. "You know, I think we should have this framed."

"Yes!" Mom said. "We'll hang it in the living room."

"Hey," I protested, but I was pleased.

The moment was ruined by Gary, who slammed open the back door and slammed it shut again.

"Hi, Grandma," he said. "Did you know that Snickers threw up on your steps again?" He took a long look at me. "What happened to you?"

Mom held up the sketch. "Look at this," she said.

Gary gawked, first at the sketch, then at me, then back at the sketch. "But you're pretty!" he yelled incredulously. He sounded disappointed.

I can't describe the satisfaction I got out of *that*.

A great day like that should have ended in some great way, but it didn't. I got a very strange long distance phone call that evening—from Jill Warren.

"How are you?" I asked, startled at hearing her voice.

She was silent for a moment, and then she said, "Actually, I'm not so great, Ceegee."

"What's wrong?" I asked. "Are you sick?"

More silence.

"Jill, you're scaring me," I said. "Has something happened?"

She began crying, hard. "I guess I just needed somebody to talk to," she said. "My folks went to a meeting, and my brother isn't home either, and Luke is spending the evening at his grandmother's house . . ."

"But what's wrong?" I asked. "If you're sick, can't you call your Uncle Duffy? He could take you to a doctor or something."

"I'm not sick like that," she said. "I'm sick of— of everything! Of that rotten Maggie Tracey and the mean things she said about my uncle . . ." She stopped talking suddenly.

"What things?" I asked quickly. I'd had a hunch the Traceys hadn't liked darling Uncle Duffy, but what could have been so terrible that Jill would cry like this?

"It's bad enough that she said what she said, but she told her crummy, stupid, ugly cousin and she goes to my school, and I'm afraid she'll tell everybody everything! And Duffy is the nicest uncle anybody ever had and it isn't fair!"

I wanted to ask her what Maggie had told her cousin, but I had a strong hunch that Jill wasn't about to answer a question like that, so instead I said, "If Maggie's cousin is anything like her, everybody in your school hates her so much that they don't care what she says."

"Maybe," she said. "Look, I'm sorry I bothered you. It was dumb. But I had to talk to somebody who knew what it was like to have everything spoiled by Maggie."

"Believe me, I know all about it," I said. "I've spent the worst weeks of my life trying to forget her."

"I wish I could," Jill said.

We talked for a little while, and then, after she promised that we'd get together sometime, she hung up.

I went to my room and looked in my mirror.

All I saw was my nose.

Maybe I could hang the sketch Mrs. Crawford made of me on the porch to scare away trick-or-treaters on Halloween.

Chapter Eleven

I was right back where I started, hating myself, my nose, and even my new school. Over the next few days, I seemed to collect hurt feelings there. After a while, I hated getting up in the morning because I knew what was coming.

For instance, two girls in the cafeteria whispered behind their hands and stared at me during lunch one day, and I left the room in tears. I'd always hated people who did that, and I was certain they'd been laughing at me.

Another time, a girl standing next to me in front of the mirror in one of the school johns asked me why I wore my hair hanging over my eyes, and I knew that she was waiting for me to confess that I was trying to hide my nose. I said, "Oh, shut up," instead, and ran out.

A short, skinny boy bumped into me in the main hall one afternoon and said, "Get out of my way, ugly." Every time I saw him after that, which seemed to be practically every five seconds, my face burned.

A substitute teacher, calling roll, stopped dead when she got to my name and said, "Isn't there an island somewhere called Caledonia?"

"Don't you mean Sardinia?" a boy with red hair asked, snickering.

"Ceegee Sardine!" somebody else yelled, and everybody laughed. After that, half the kids in the class called me Sardine for the rest of the week.

Starting middle school hadn't done much for my self-confidence anyway, but all this was making me so miserable that I seriously considered running away, but I couldn't decide where to go and I knew I'd miss my family. Except for Gary, of course.

Molly was having serious troubles, too. She gained four pounds in September, another four in October (she blamed that on her Halloween party), and by November the two of us were ready to try getting lost on our way to school every morning. Unfortunately, we were too old to lose our way in our own neighborhood.

One day in the cafeteria, while rain poured down outside, Molly, Bernadette, Dina, and I made plans for meeting at a big shopping mall on the day after Thanksgiving for lunch and a little early Christmas shopping.

"We're going to have a real lunch this time," Molly said. "Last time we got together, you guys didn't have any fun at all because I made you eat in that awful vegetarian place and I still gained at least three tons. Tomorrow we really eat!"

"I can't afford a real lunch," Dina said. "I've got to save every cent for Christmas."

"It's going to be my treat, everybody," I said. "I earned a small fortune helping Grandma clean out her closets last weekend. I'm practically rich."

"Are you sure you want to do this?" Dina asked.

"I'm sure," I said. "It's going to be fun."

I was wrong.

The other girls and I had met outside the restaurant at eleven-thirty, and by noon, our orders were sitting on the table in front of us.

Molly smiled down on her chili burger, fries, and chocolate shake. "This is paradise," she said. "I'll make up for it by starving tomorrow."

"Yum," Bernadette said, and she bit into her bacon burger on a sourdough bun.

"Heavenly," Dina said, picking up her triple-decker chicken, avocado, and tomato sandwich.

"Well, well," a voice said. "Look who's here."

I gawked and flinched. There stood Maggie Tracey, smiling down on me while half the insides of my hamburger oozed out of the bun and plopped on my plate.

She was wearing an absolutely gorgeous jacket that must have cost more than my entire school wardrobe. Her pale blond hair was shiny and perfect. Her skin glowed. Her eyelashes were long, black, and curly. She was beautiful, looked as if she was at least sixteen, and I hated her so much that the mouthful of food I was trying to swallow turned to stone.

I choked and coughed, and finally managed to say, "Hello, Maggie."

She smiled at the other girls at my table. "What happened to your manners, Ceegee?" she said to me. "Introduce me to your friends."

I could tell from the expression on Molly's face that she recognized Maggie from the snapshots Chris had taken at the picnic last August. But she pretended not to hear Maggie's name when I said it.

"I'm glad to meet you, Agnes," Molly said. "Sorry there isn't room for you at the table, so maybe we'll see you some other time, but probably not." And she took another big bite out of her chili burger.

Maggie blinked, but her big, phony smile didn't fade. She looked at the other girls. "So nice meeting you, Dina. You, too, Bernadette."

Bernadette must have been a mind reader. I'd never told her much about Maggie, but she picked up on my misery instantly, the way a good friend would.

"Ceegee has never mentioned you," she said to Maggie in a loud, huffy voice, as if she wanted proof that Maggie really knew me. "Are you somebody from her elementary school?"

"We have the same birthday," Maggie said. "Didn't Ceegee tell you about our birthday picnic?"

"I guess I forgot," I said.

"We'll have to get together sometime and talk about it," Maggie said. "What's happened to your

104

hair? How sad, Ceegee. I thought last summer that you had fairly nice hair."

"Hey," Dina protested, and she tossed her sandwich down. "That was a rotten thing to say."

"Oh, there's my friend," Maggie exclaimed, and she waved at someone across the restaurant. "So nice talking to you," she murmured vaguely, and she hurried away.

I looked down at the remains of my hamburger. "I suppose if I dropped dead right here and now, I'd embarrass you guys even worse than I already have."

"You didn't embarrass us," Bernadette said. "But she—what's-her-name—is the biggest jerk I ever met. How dare she stand over us like that and make that nasty remark about your hair! Who does she think she is?"

"She thinks she's Maggie Tracey," I said, glum and miserable. "And we're not."

"Why didn't you wear your hair brushed back and your grandmother's earrings?" Bernadette demanded. "You'd have knocked her dead."

"I know I look awful now," I said apologetically.

"You do not look awful!" Bernadette shouted. "You look like everybody else, that's all. Why not look terrific and glamorous and mysterious if you can? That would have shown Maggie."

No, I thought. She wouldn't have cared, because even with my hair back and wearing Grandma's earrings, I still wasn't gorgeous. And even if I'd been gorgeous, it still wouldn't have been enough. I had no idea what would have been enough, either.

*   *   *

I didn't enjoy lunch or shopping afterward. I stared at myself in every mirror I saw. And I asked myself over and over what was wrong with me.

I had a hunch it wasn't just my nose. There was something about my attitude that wasn't right. I didn't have whatever my Aunt Cally had. And I didn't know how to get it.

I got home in the middle of the afternoon and found Grandma and Gary in the kitchen fixing a meal for Snickers.

"What did you get me for Christmas?" Gary asked, getting right to the point, as he usually did.

"Nothing," I said. I took a handful of crackers out of the box on the counter and sat down on a stool. "But I've decided what I'm going to get you next time I go shopping."

"What?" Gary asked.

"Something you'll hate," I told him. I fed a cracker to Snickers.

"Somebody called you when you were gone, but I forget who," Gary said.

Grandma interrupted him. "Chris called you, Ceegee. He wants you to call him back."

"Chris?" I asked stupidly. "Chris from the picnic?"

"Chris, the photographer," Grandma corrected. She couldn't stand thinking about the picnic, either. "I took the call and wrote down his number, there by the phone."

She put Snickers' bowl on the floor. Snickers looked from the bowl to her and then back to the bowl again, as if he couldn't believe what he saw. Then he hustled over to me and begged for another cracker. I gave him one. Why should there be more than one miserable person in the house?

"Are you going to call Chris?" Gary asked.

"What did he want?" I asked Grandma suspiciously.

Grandma shrugged. "Maybe he only wants to have a chat with a friend."

"I saw Maggie today," I said. "One conversation with somebody from the picnic is enough."

"You saw Maggie?" Grandma asked, and she seemed genuinely astonished. "Good grief, I thought she and her mother probably had gotten rained on and melted into little piles of ashes."

"Not all witches can be killed with water," Gary said solemnly. "Sometimes you have to stab them with wooden stakes."

"Quick, Igor, hand me a stake," I grumbled.

"Enough with the jokes," Grandma said. "Tell me where you saw Maggie and what happened."

"She came into the restaurant where we were having lunch and told me that my hair looks terrible," I said.

"It does not!" Gary cried, and then realized what he'd just said and added, "Well, not too terrible."

"Thank you," I said, sincerely grateful to the little creep.

"I hope you answered her back appropriately,"

107

Grandma said. She didn't believe in letting anybody get away with anything.

"No, I choked on my food instead," I said. "Let's face it, I'm hopeless. The only time I can think up snotty things to say is in the middle of the night when nobody cares."

"You can call them then," Gary said earnestly. "That's what I do."

"What?" Grandma shouted. "You call people in the middle of the night?"

"Well, only a couple of times," Gary admitted.

"Good for you," Grandma said. "But there's no reason to blab this interesting information around the dinner table, if you get my meaning, pal."

"You're terrific, Grandma," Gary said. "Mom would kill me. Ceegee, are you going to call Chris now?"

"No," I said. "I don't know what he wants and I'm afraid to find out."

"He doesn't care about your hair or even your nose," Gary said generously.

I glared at him. "I like you better when you're not trying to be nice," I said.

"Go call," Grandma said. "Your parents will be home soon and then we'll be starting dinner. Call."

I did, although I didn't want to talk to Chris, mainly because I didn't already know what he wanted. Conversations with people who are practically strangers are always easier if you have some idea of what they want.

He answered his phone on the second ring.

"Chris? It's Ceegee."

108

"Yo, Ceegee," he said happily. "I thought maybe you weren't going to call me back."

"I just got home," I said. "What do you want?" Like Gary, I could get straight to the point.

"I won a prize for one of the pictures I took at the picnic," he said. "First prize, in the Seattle Middle School Camera Club Contest. Ten dollars and two dozen rolls of film. How about that?"

"That's wonderful," I said, meaning it. "I told you that you were a good photographer. Which picture was it?"

"The one of you, Nancy Penn, and Jill Warren's Uncle Duffy. Remember? The three of you were standing on the shore looking across the lake, and the sun was just right, and the shadows fell right, and . . ."

"And somebody with talent snapped the picture," I said. "Congratulations. I never knew anybody before who won a prize for taking a photograph. That was one of my favorites."

"Good," he said. "You know which one I liked best?"

"Which one?"

"The one that Duffy took of you and me sitting on the table under the big tree. My braces didn't show." And he laughed.

Boys care about things like that? I was amazed. "That was a good picture," I said.

"I enlarged it," Chris said. "I sent it to my aunt in California."

"I bet she liked it, too."

"She wanted to know who the cute girl was," he said. "I told her you were lots better than just

109

a cute girl. I told her that you play really good softball. So does she, so she was impressed. And I told her you had a great sense of humor."

The hand I was using to hold the phone went numb.

Somebody thought I was *more* than just a cute girl?

I wasn't cute. But I played great softball.

And I did have a sense of humor. Who could survive my family without one?

Who could survive Maggie without one?

This conversation was making me feel better, but it was embarrassing, too, so I changed the subject.

"Have you seen Rod lately?" I asked.

"Sure," Chris said. "I'm going skiing with his family next weekend. We're both glad your mother set up that picnic, because otherwise we probably never would have met. Do you ever see any of the girls?"

"I've talked to both Jill and Nancy, but we haven't done anything about getting together."

"You should," Chris said. "Who knows? Maybe next year we can have another birthday picnic."

"Maybe," I said doubtfully. "I didn't like the picnic all that much. But not because of you or Rod, or your parents. It was something else."

"Yeah," Chris said. "That Maggie. Gee, my mom was so mad that she griped about Maggie for weeks afterward. She said that Maggie and her mother ruined everything. I'm not sure Mom would go to another picnic, and that's too bad. Some of us had fun, most of the time, that is."

"Part of the time," I said.

After we hung up, I realized that if Chris had been a girl, I'd have told him how much Maggie hurt me. But boys don't seem to get as bent out of shape over things as girls. At least, if they do, they find a way of dealing with their feelings.

Like my brother calling up his enemies in the middle of the night.

What a brat.

What a great idea.

But I knew I'd never do it. No, I'd just lie awake worrying about running into Maggie again and wondering what was wrong with me. Aside from my nose and my name, of course.

It helped knowing that Chris thought I played good ball and had a sense of humor. Maybe I needed to write out a list of things I was good at, instead of always going over the bad things in my mind.

That night before I went to bed, I wrote out the list. It went like this:

Ceegee's Good Points, Talents, and Admirable Qualities

1. Good softball player.
2. Good sense of humor.
3. Still hasn't murdered her brother.
4. Does most of her homework on time.
5. Remembers to fill the dog's water dish.

I was beginning to feel a little desperate to fill the list, too.

6. Saves part of her allowance.
7. Never sasses grown-ups (well, hardly ever).
8. Looks pretty good with her hair brushed back and wearing her grandmother's earrings.

I read that last one over in surprise, because I could hardly believe I wrote it. Did I mean it? There was only one way to find out.

Chapter Twelve

Changing how you look is easy. What's hard is changing how you *feel* about how you look. No matter what I told myself, a mean little voice in the back of my mind repeated over and over that I was kidding myself. You can dress a macaw up in a fur coat, but she won't look like a pretty little rabbit. She'll look like a macaw acting like an idiot.

I spent a long time fussing with my hair the next morning. I brushed it straight back and fastened it with a big clip. Then I put on Grandma's wonderful earrings. I'd already dressed in the skirt and vest that I hadn't dared to wear since Mom and I bought them. At first glance, it seemed to me that I looked taller, not skinnier.

At second glance, I was only Ceegee wearing new clothes that made her look weird.

But something else wasn't right, either, the little voice said. I didn't look the way I had the day I posed for the art class. What was wrong?

A scarf! Yes. I rummaged through my drawers until I found a long, striped one. It took several tries before I succeeded in winding it around my head the way Mrs. Crawford had. Then I stepped back from the mirror so I could study the result.

I can't go to school this way, I thought. My nose is still there. All of it. Only now my swamp-colored eyes showed worse than ever.

The little voice said, "You're right about that."

Also, I looked—I don't know—like somebody else. I seemed older and taller and almost as if I had some sort of sassy self-confidence—which was a big lie, of course. In other words, I did not look much like Caledonia MacBride, the world's biggest joke. *I was a fake*. And that made me uncomfortable. How many other people would notice that I was pretending to be somebody different? And how many of them were going to get a very big laugh over it?

"Ceegee, you're late for breakfast!" Mom shouted up the stairs.

I reached for the scarf, to pull it off and stuff it back in the drawer. But something stopped me.

Mrs. Crawford had told me that I'd be more beautiful every year of my life. Of course, I knew she didn't mean it. Nobody could be that dim-witted. But maybe she really meant that I was truly different and that was a good thing.

Maybe. She might have been feeling sorry for me, too.

"Ceegee!"

Too late. I didn't have time to coax curls back

into my hair and pull down my bangs now. I walked slowly downstairs, prepared for the worst.

At the table, my father glanced up at me over the top of his newspaper, but only for a second. "You look as if you had a good night's sleep," he said. Then he turned back to the classifieds and read aloud one about someone selling eight antique sinks, cheap, you haul.

Gary, spooning canned peaches over his mayonnaise sandwich, said, "Did you take my School Stinks tee shirt, Ceegee? I wanted to wear it but I can't find it, and I looked everywhere. You better not be hiding it."

I sat down and helped myself to scrambled eggs. "I don't have your School Stinks tee shirt. Maybe Mom threw it out with the rest of the trash."

Mom, shoving bread in the toaster, said nothing.

"Mom?" Gary asked. "Did you throw it out? Did you?"

Mom shrugged. "Not exactly. I had a small accident while I was doing the laundry and that tee shirt accidentally got bleach spilled on it. You can't read the letters anymore. What a terrible shame."

Dad lowered the paper again. "Quit while you're ahead," he said to Gary.

"I paid Donny two bucks for that tee shirt!" Gary complained. "It was hardly even used."

Mom sat down and took a sip of her orange juice. "Ceegee, if you're coming straight home after school, would you empty the dishwasher? I won't have time this morning. And by the way, I like your hair."

"Sure." My hair. At last somebody noticed something. But she didn't say I looked different and terrific and mysterious. Or older and taller and exciting.

Grandma stuck her head in the back door. "Ceegee, do you want a ride to school? I'm driving that way this morning."

"I'm not ready to leave yet, Grandma, but thanks anyway." Snickers leaned against my leg and moaned hopefully. I passed him a bit of toast.

"Don't feed the dog at the table," Dad said automatically, without looking away from the paper. "He's getting too fat. He waddles when he walks."

Snickers bared his teeth in a silent snarl.

"I love seeing those earrings on you," Grandma said, "especially with your hair pulled back." Then she shut the door.

Gary looked straight at me and blinked, as if seeing me for the first time. "Aw, jeez," he said. "You look like you're going to a party or something dumb like that."

My parents both stared.

"Do I?" I asked, worried. I hadn't meant to go that far. Terrific and wonderful and mysterious are not the same as being dressed up for a party.

"Well, the scarf's fine, but the real gold earrings are a bit much for school," Mom said slowly. "They're awfully valuable. You'd feel bad if you lost one."

"I won't!" I said. I didn't have courage for the

hairdo and scarf unless I was wearing the earrings.

Mom transferred her stare to Gary. "Maybe somebody I know ought to give Ceegee an early Christmas present."

"What?" Gary cried. "Are you talking to me?"

"Nobody else," Mom said. "I think the time is right."

"Do I have to get her another present?" Gary demanded.

"No," Mom said. "Ceegee will understand."

"I don't understand any of this!" I cried. "What are you talking about?"

"Gary thinks he should give you his Christmas gift now," Mom said, even though it was clear from the expression on Gary's face that he didn't share her opinion.

"I'm not giving you anything else," Gary said to me as he got up from the table.

While he ran upstairs and back down again, I pestered Mom for an explanation, but she wouldn't tell me a thing. Gary came in and shoved a small box at me.

"Here," he said. "Merry Christmas."

Bewildered, I opened the box. Inside I found a pair of gold-colored earrings with nickle-sized disks hanging from short chains. Each had the face of a smiling cat on it. They were so cute that I could hardly believe Gary had picked them out.

"I love them," I said, meaning it.

"I tried to find some with parrots on them, but they didn't have any," Gary said, doing his best to ruin the moment.

"He did not," Mom said. "As soon as he saw these, he said he had to get them for you, even though they cost more than he could really afford."

I gawked at my brother. He glared down at his plate and scratched his elbow.

"Thank you very much, Gary," I said. "This is the nicest early Christmas present I ever got."

"It's the *only* one you ever got," he grumbled.

I changed earrings and ran to the hall mirror to see what I looked like. Oh, the earrings were wonderful. And they didn't look like I was going to a party. There were other girls at school who had animal earrings, some even carved out of wood.

But still, nobody had mentioned how different I looked. What was the matter with my family? Didn't they notice how much work I'd gone to, making myself over?

When I met Molly at the corner, she was impressed with the earrings, too. "They look terrific. I can't believe Gary came up with an idea like that."

"Neither can I, but he did. Maybe there's some hope for him after all."

"I wouldn't get all bent out of shape over it," Molly said, cautioning me. "Remember, we're talking about Gary MacBride, your brother."

I laughed. And then I remembered that Molly didn't comment about my hair, either.

"How does my hair look?"

She studied me carefully. "I like it. It suits you. And it shows off the earrings."

Well, that was nice, but she hadn't fallen over in a faint over the new Ceegee.

I waited all morning, through one class after another, for someone, anyone, to comment about the big change. All anybody wanted to talk about was my earrings. I could have looked like the old Ceegee, for all anybody else cared. But at least none of the boys called me ugly.

However, once, while I was glaring at myself in the mirror in the john, the girl who had once asked me why I wore my hair in my eyes said, "I like what you did with the scarf. I think I'll try that myself."

"Thanks," I muttered.

It wasn't until I reached my art class that the new Ceegee got any real attention.

"Hey," the girl in front of me said, "you're wearing your hair the same way you did when you were the class model. It shows off your cheekbones and your eyes, like Mrs. Crawford said. You really look great."

A couple of other kids glanced over at me then. I could practically read their minds while they imagined drawing my face, even my nose. Finally Mrs. Crawford noticed me. And she smiled a big smile.

Before that class was over, at least half the girls stopped by my table to comment about the scarf, the earrings—and my hair. And the change in me.

"You seem older like this," one girl said. "You look like a real model. Or somebody else special."

119

What's happening? I asked myself. Why are they noticing *me* here and not anywhere else?

Bernadette gave me the answer.

As we were leaving the room, she said, "It wasn't until we got to art that I really looked at you, Ceegee. I guess this is the only place where my eyes are connected to my brain. You look so different. I love your hair like that, with the scarf wrapped around it. And the big earrings are perfect. Altogether, I love what I see."

"Hardly anybody else outside of art noticed anything but the earrings," I said.

"Nobody else has had Mrs. Crawford to teach them how to see," she said. "Probably the others just notice that you look different, but they can't figure out all the reasons why. That's a good kind of attention. It means you did a wonderful job."

I felt relieved. "But do I actually look better?" I asked Bernadette.

She considered my question for almost too long. Finally she said, "It's not that you look better. It's that you look—I don't know—satisfied with yourself. You look like my cat right after she washes her whiskers. Does that make sense?"

"In a very weird way," I said, laughing. "But I feel like a fake. The real Ceegee has awful hair, a big nose, and bones sticking out in all the wrong places. All those dumb things are still here."

She shook her head. "No way, Ceegee. This is the real you. I can *see* that."

I rushed to my next class smiling. It was almost as if Bernadette and I, and the others in the art class, shared a secret way of looking at the world and ourselves. We knew how to look for more than what was ordinary. And if something was lacking, we were beginning to learn how to supply it.

I, Caledonia Giorsa MacBride, big nose and all, was more than ordinary. And the little voice in the back of my mind was satisfied. For the time being, anyway.

I sent Christmas cards to all the birthday kids except Maggie, and I included notes in two of them. I invited both Jill and Nancy to have lunch with me in downtown Seattle two days after Christmas. I wasn't sure Jill could make it, because she lived in North Valley, but I got a card back from her with a note scribbled inside.

"I'll be there! My mother will drive me into town and visit some friends of hers while we have lunch. Tell Nancy I can hardly wait."

Nancy phoned me as soon as she got her card, and she, too, was excited about meeting again after all these months. She sounded happy, which was nice. Maybe she, too, was recovering from that awful birthday picnic last August.

Christmas was great, as usual, even though Dad gave Snickers a dog treat that he hated and chewed up in little pieces all over Dad's favorite chair. On the day after Christmas Grandma left for her winter vacation in Hawaii, and on the day after that I dressed up in my new Christmas clothes, brushed back my hair, put on my now-famous cat earrings, and went downtown to meet my birthday pals.

Both of them were on time. Jill, grinning, said, "Boy, do you look great, Ceegee. You seem taller or something."

I smiled to myself. "Maybe I am."

"Great earrings," Nancy said. "I've got some with elephants. I wish I'd worn them."

We ordered lunch and while we were waiting for our food, we talked about our schools.

"Boring but bearable," Nancy said. "Rod says to tell you hello."

"I almost like my school," Jill said, "but not quite. "My Uncle Duffy says to regard it as only a pothole on the road of life."

We all laughed at that. "Duffy was the best part of the picnic," Nancy said, "except for meeting the two of you."

"Well, Chris and Rod aren't so bad," Jill said.

"It's Maggie who was the clinker," I said. Suddenly I realized that I'd said her name out loud and hadn't developed a stomachache at the same time. I told the others that.

"Maybe we're getting over her," Jill said.

"Is it possible?" Nancy asked. "That's almost like getting over terminal warts."

"Wouldn't she be jealous if she knew that the three of us were having lunch together and never even thought of inviting her?" I asked.

"Oh, yes!" Jill breathed. "If only there was some way of letting her know."

"There's a phone by the door we came in through," I said. "We could call her."

"Good grief, no," Nancy said. "She might show up during dessert. We should have asked Chris to drop by and take a picture of us sitting here, having a good time."

The waitress brought our food, and we began eating. Suddenly I had the idea of a lifetime.

"Listen," I said, "there's a place on the next block, a big drugstore, that has one of those photo booths in it. You know, you sit inside, feed it some money, and it takes your picture."

"Let's go there when we're done eating," Jill said.

"We'll all get in the booth together and send the picture to Maggie," Nancy said.

"With a belated Christmas card," I said. "We'll say we suddenly remembered her and wanted her to know we were thinking about her and isn't it too bad she missed out on our holiday lunch."

"Yeah," Jill said, grinning. "Too bad."

We enjoyed our lunch, had big desserts, traded all our good news—and there was plenty—and made plans to meet again as soon as we could. Each of us, in one way or another, had come to terms with what rotten Maggie had done to us. Not that we forgave her, of course. We definitely weren't saints.

We didn't make plans for another birthday picnic, though. That would have been expecting too much of us so soon. But we were going to keep in touch.

And who knows, I told myself. Maybe someday I can even face up to another joint birthday—as long as it didn't include Maggie.

Then we marched off together to have our photograph taken.

It turned out wonderfully well. I sat on one side with my profile showing, and I was wearing a huge grin. Jill faced me, also grinning. And Nancy sat staring straight at the camera. I wish I could say that she was grinning, but the awful truth was that she was sticking out her tongue. Like I said, we weren't saints.

We found the Traceys' address in the phone book, but instead of a Christmas card, we sent the photo in a New Year's card, wishing Maggie everything she deserved.

And we signed it, "The Birthday Girls."